A VALENTINE CONFESSION

"You must not worry on my account, Stephen."

"But I will worry, Vanessa." Stephen's arm tightened around her and he pulled her even closer. "You must know you are very dear to me."

Vanessa took a shivering breath. Dared she voice what was in her heart? He appeared to be waiting for her answer, and Vanessa found she could not disappoint him. "I share your sentiments, Stephen. You are also very dear to me."

"I have waited long years to hear those very words." He smiled, his first genuine smile, and gathered her in a close embrace. "I must be honest with you, my dear, for my heart is heavy with this burden."

Vanessa stared up at him in surprise, trembling slightly at the pleasure of his embrace. Her lips parted in wonder, and before she could think to pull back, he lowered his lips to hers and kissed her. . . .

Books by Kathryn Kirkwood

A MATCH FOR MELISSA
A SEASON FOR SAMANTHA
A HUSBAND FOR HOLLY
A VALENTINE FOR VANESSA

Published by Zebra Books

A VALENTINE FOR VANESSA

Kathryn Kirkwood

Zebra Books
Kensington Publishing Corp.

http://www.zebrabooks.com

ZEBRA BOOKS are published by

Kensington Publishing Corp.
850 Third Avenue
New York, NY 10022

Zebra and the Z logo Reg. U.S. Pat. & TM Off.

First Printing: January, 2000
10 9 8 7 6 5 4 3 2 1

Printed in the United States of America

For Bob & Dimmi—
Good friends, staunch supporters, and great chiropractors

One

Vanessa Elizabeth Holland smiled as her papa opened the door for her. She carried a parcel containing his latest manuscript, *The Compleat and Illustrated Guide to Medicinal Botanicals*, and she had faithfully promised to execute the illustrations before the end of the year.

She would have to work quickly, but she had begun her drawings the previous spring, the moment her subjects had leafed out, and had only a few left to render. At times in the past several years, she had burned her candle into the wee hours of the morning, but had never failed to accomplish her share of the work on time.

"Take a care, Vanessa," Mr. Holland called out.

Vanessa ducked her head as she exited the cottage. Her father followed, also stooping as he went through the doorway, and together they stepped out into the November air. It was a lovely morning in Martin's Summer, the brief period of unseasonably balmy days that prompts one to hope the weather might hold. But Vanessa sensed the barest hint of frost in the air. The English winter would arrive shortly, with its cold wet days, fierce winds, and blankets of heavy snow.

"Has the doorway grown shorter, or have I grown taller?" Vanessa turned to her father and grinned.

"Neither, my dear. You have simply become accustomed

to your accommodations at Bridgeford Hall. The doorways there have much more height."

"True, and it is a luxury to enter a chamber without fear of coshing my head against the top of the doorframe. Do you know the story of how the doorways came to be so uncommonly tall?"

Mr. Holland shook his head and took a seat on the bench by the door in anticipation of a good story. Vanessa sat down beside him and smiled.

"It seems Stephen's grandfather, the seventh Earl of Bridgeford, had the doorways raised as his first official act. His countess was several inches taller than he, and had to stoop to enter all but the grand dining hall and the ballroom."

"How tall was the countess?"

Vanessa shrugged. "Stephen was not certain precisely, but said his grandmother easily equaled my height."

"Then she was quite tall for the times."

"Yes, indeed." Vanessa nodded. "And her son, Stephen's father, grew to be an inch taller than his mother. When Stephen was born years later, his grandmother took his measure on his second birthday and predicted he would grow even taller than his father. She was correct—he exceeded his father's height by a full three inches."

Mr. Holland chuckled. "The earl's height is indeed remarkable. When he came back to claim his title, he also claimed *my* title as the tallest man in Bridgeford Valley. It makes one wonder how his sister came to be so petite."

"The very same thought crossed my mind." Vanessa laughed, thinking of the contrast between the uncommonly tall earl and his diminutive sister. "When I asked him about it, he said Millie resembles his mother's side of the family. The Hampton ladies are quite dainty. I find it most intriguing how physical characteristics can be passed down to a couple's offspring. If there were only some way to predict the outcome, we could nurture the desirable elements and eliminate the undesirable."

Mr. Holland chuckled. "Ah, but that is a dangerous subject. One would have to decide which characteristics are desirable and which are not. I daresay it is better left to chance or, as the rector would claim, to God."

"Since you have mentioned the rector, I will remind you once again of your promise to collect his daughter and carry her with you when you come for tea this afternoon. Millie will enjoy making her acquaintance."

"I won't forget, dear." Geoffrey Holland held up his finger, around which Vanessa had tied a bit of colored string. "I have this to remind me, in addition to the notes you have left in every corner of the cottage."

Vanessa's laughter echoed in the early morning air. She had posted reminders in her father's study, his kitchen, his bedchamber, and even on the inside of the cottage door, where he would be certain to see it before he took his leave. "Do you suspect I have reminded you overmuch, Papa?"

"Perhaps not." A bemused smile spread across Mr. Holland's face. "I am regrettably absentminded at times, especially when I am engrossed in my research. If it were not for Mrs. Carstairs, I suspect I should forget to eat."

Vanessa shook her head, her curly blond hair escaping from the bun she had fashioned at the nape of her neck. "You need have no fear on that score. If you gave the slightest appearance of losing flesh, every widow in Bridgeford Village would arrive at your door with treats from her table. You may not regard yourself as a handsome, eligible widower, but I assure you they do."

"I expect you have the right of it, my dear." A wry smile crossed Mr. Holland's lips. "The Widow Moorehouse arrived only yesterday morning with a basket of tarts she had baked. She said I looked a bit pulled, and she worried Mrs. Carstairs was neglecting me. Of course, she stated that her true reason for interrupting my work was to deliver a letter that had arrived in the post, but I am certain that . . ."

"What is it, Papa?" Vanessa frowned as her father abruptly stopped speaking.

"I *am* regrettably forgetful!" Mr. Holland reached into his pocket to draw out a crumpled letter. "And here is the proof. The letter Widow Moorehouse brought was for you. I believe it is from your friend at Lackington's Bookshop."

"Yes, it appears so." Vanessa glanced at the letter and thrust it into the pocket of her cape. She felt her face flame and she turned away to hide her reaction from her father.

"I think it uncommonly nice of the young man to send you word of new publications. I am certain no other employee would be so thoughtful. Perhaps you should arrange to meet with him personally to discuss which of his offerings might best appeal to Lady Thurston and her brother."

"Why?" Vanessa pretended great interest in a heavily laden cart lumbering along the road.

"He is admirably faithful in his correspondence, and you have a common interest. Many affairs of the heart are based on far less."

The twinkle in her father's eye warned her she was in for a bit of teasing. "Please, Papa. I know nothing about this London gentleman, nor do I wish to. You are well on your way to concocting a soup from naught but water and salt."

"Perhaps I am." Mr. Holland nodded. "But you would make an excellent wife and mother, Vanessa, and I should like to see you happily settled before I grow too old to enjoy my grandchildren. Is there not a young man in all of England you find appealing?"

Laughing, Vanessa hugged her father. "There are a

great many appealing young men, Papa, but few would court a miss soon to celebrate her twenty-sixth birthday. And you must not forget that I tower over most eligible gentleman by several inches. Only a man who equals your stature would suit me, Papa, and I have met no such gentleman."

"Only the earl," Mr. Holland pointed out. "It is a great pity he is already married. The two of you would suit very well."

Vanessa turned away again to hide the color that burned in her cheeks. She had often thought the same, but it would not be proper of her to divulge it. Though Stephen's wife was not in residence at Bridgeford Hall, forming a *tendre* for a married gentleman would be foolish. Even if Stephen were a bachelor, it was unlikely a gentleman of the peerage would choose a wife so far beneath him in status.

Mr. Holland took her hand. "You must not despair, Vanessa. Your mother used to say that for every lady there is a gentleman, and you are no exception. While it is true your proportions are statuesque, you are a true beauty in the classical sense of the word. Someone will capture your heart. You will see."

Vanessa leaned close to kiss her father on the cheek. He had always been her staunch supporter, telling her to pay no mind when her friends, each far smaller and daintier, had been courted and led off to the altar.

"Are you unhappy?" Mr. Holland drew back to look into his daughter's deep green eyes.

"Unhappy?" Vanessa shook her head. "No, Papa. How could I be unhappy? You, Millie, and a large group of friends hold me in great esteem. I am auntie to all my friends' children and I never lack for companionship."

"And that is enough?"

"Indeed." Vanessa hoped her father would not notice the hint of sadness in her eyes.

Her answer seemed to satisfy him, and Mr. Holland released her with a fond pat. "I believe I hear the earl's carriage. You had best gather your things and be off. But do not dismiss the suggestion I made concerning the young man from Lackington's Bookshop. It is possible he is the very gentleman for you."

"Yes, Papa." Vanessa retrieved the bundled manuscript and the large wicker basket, now empty of the fine repast she had brought from Bridgeford Hall's kitchens. The earl's carriage had arrived fortuitously, for she did not wish to discuss her letters. She had never been less than truthful with her father, but she had spun a Banbury tale regarding the letters she received. In truth, Vanessa had to lie to her beloved parent. Mr. Holland would be overset if he knew the letters contained words of love and had not been written by an employee of Lackington's Bookshop. He would surely have an attack of apoplexy if he suspected Vanessa had not a clue to the identity of the gentleman who wrote the private and passionate words.

As the coach drew up, Mr. Holland greeted the elderly driver with a smile. "Hello, John. What do your bones tell you of the weather?"

"It's changing, Doc." John used the name the villagers had given Mr. Holland by virtue of his apothecary work. "My leg's starting to twinge something fierce. Rain's coming. You can be sure of that!"

Mr. Holland nodded. "You'd best have Cook brew you some willow bark tea. One cup three times a day, and you'll be spared most of the discomfort."

"Worked like a charm the last time, it did." John grinned, showing several gaps in his teeth. "Now if you could only make a potion to help me sleep at night, I'd be a happy man. Every time I get settled in bed, peaceful like, the wife wakes me up with another piece of gossip."

Vanessa laughed, knowing full well how John's wife, Ellie, could run on. She was one of the maids at Bridgeford

Hall, and her tongue often wagged more rapidly than her dusting cloth. "Perhaps some lobelia tea would be in order. What do you think, Papa?"

"An excellent suggestion!" Mr. Holland winked at his daughter. "I'll bring a packet to your wife when I come to tea at Bridgeford Hall and instruct her in how to prepare it."

The coachman nodded. "I should drink it before I retire for the night?"

"No, John." Vanessa laughed merrily. "Your *wife* should drink it."

John looked confused. "But how will that help me sleep?"

"It will slow your wife's tongue," Mr. Holland said, "and once she is asleep, you will be able to do the same."

John caught their meaning immediately and a grin spread over his face. "No doubt that'll do the trick. Let me help you with your baggage, Miss Vanessa."

"I have it, John." Vanessa stopped the elderly coachman as he made to climb down from the bench. She placed her basket and the wrapped manuscript on the seat of the coach and turned to her father for one final word. "Good-bye, Papa. Please do not forget to . . ."

Mr. Holland stopped another reminder by holding up his finger. "I will not fail to arrive at teatime with Miss Prudence in tow."

"Thank you." Vanessa smiled. "Perhaps you should put the packet of lobelia leaves in your pocket now, so John will be assured of a restful night's sleep."

"An excellent suggestion, and one I will follow the moment John has carried you away."

Vanessa climbed into the carriage and John clucked softly to the horses. Soon they were traveling up the familiar road to Bridgeford Hall.

Vanessa leaned back against the padded squabs with a sigh. She hoped Millie had not missed her too much in the day she had spent away from the Hall. When Vanessa had first taken up her position as companion to the earl's sister, Millie broke down in tears every time Vanessa left her side. Now, after three years, Millie was much more self-assured. Yesterday morning when Vanessa prepared to leave the Hall, Millie actually smiled in anticipation of the plans she had made to occupy her time in Vanessa's absence.

"Had the earl returned when you left?" Vanessa leaned out the window to query the coachman.

"I passed him at the gates, Miss Vanessa." John leaned down from the box to answer her. "He pulled up his horse to tell me he was late for a meeting with his agent, and he said to tell you he would join you and Lady Thurston for dinner."

"Thank you, John." Vanessa sat back, smiling broadly, anticipating the lively conversation they would have over dinner. Stephen, the name he insisted she call him when she had accepted his offer of employment, would have exciting tales of his travels. He had been gone for three long months, and she had anticipated his return as much as Millie had. Now he was back. Vanessa could scarcely wait to show him how much his sister's spirits had improved in his absence.

Two

When Vanessa arrived at Bridgeford Hall, she was told Millie had just arisen and would join her in the breakfast room. "I trust Millie was in good spirits while I was gone, Mr. Welles?"

"Indeed, she was!" The elderly butler, normally staid and stodgy, chuckled slightly. "She asked Cook to teach her to bake apple tartlets."

Vanessa raised her brows at this revelation. "Apple tartlets? Whatever for?"

"I should not have said anything." Welles winced slightly. "Your father told Lady Millie they were your favorite, and she wanted them to be a surprise for your breakfast."

Vanessa grinned. "Then I will be suitably surprised, do not worry. I'll never let it slip that you told me."

"Thank you, Miss Vanessa."

"John mentioned he passed the earl at the gates." Vanessa hoped her face did not reveal her inner excitement.

Welles nodded. "His lordship arrived not more than a half hour ago. The moment I told Cook, she began to prepare his favorite homecoming meal."

"Then we are to dine on wild duck once again?" Vanessa smiled in anticipation of the tasty treat.

"Yes, and haunch of venison. The earl shares his father's love of game from his own preserves."

"But no jugged hare?" Vanessa exchanged a wink with the butler.

"Nary a trace, Miss Vanessa."

She laughed and the butler joined in. Welles had told her how fond Stephen's mother had been of jugged hare. The countess had insisted it be served with every family dinner. Stephen had grown up despising the sight of jugged hare and had ordered Cook never to prepare it when he was in residence.

"Shall I have George bring you a cup of chocolate in the breakfast room?"

"Thank you, yes."

The butler turned and hobbled off toward the kitchens. Welles had been the butler at Bridgeford Hall almost half a century, and though he was well along in years, he had told Stephen he had no wish to retire until he had outlived his usefulness.

Welles *had* outlived his usefulness, but Stephen spared the butler's sensibilities in a very clever way. When Stephen returned from his last trip to London, he'd brought along a man he called an "under butler." He assured Welles all the finer mansions in London had under butlers, and it would be Welles's task to supervise and train the man as his assistant.

Welles accepted his under butler willingly, never realizing the man had been hired specifically to lighten his workload and cause him to feel useful and necessary.

As she climbed the grand staircase, Vanessa wondered whether Stephen was in the chamber he had refurbished as his study. The earl's habit after a prolonged absence was to meet with his men of business the day he returned. She glanced in the study as she passed, and smiled. Several men sat in leather armchairs pulled close to the desk. It was comforting to know his routine had not changed. Surely if Stephen's wife had been well enough to return to England with him, he would be with her, not with his solicitors and agents.

Vanessa frowned as she rounded the corner and set off for the east wing. She should hope Stephen's wife regained her health so they could be reunited, but she could not bring herself to do so. With Stephen's wife in residence, Vanessa's position as Millie's companion might be terminated, especially if the countess noticed Vanessa's admiration for the earl. On the other hand, if the countess were wise, she would not be anxious over Vanessa's relationship to Stephen. While they were friends and partners in their concern over Millie, Stephen had never exhibited a hint of impropriety in his dealings with Vanessa. "Oh, bother!" Vanessa winced as she barked her shin on a piecrust table placed a bit further out from the wall than usual. She picked up the table, placed it back in its proper position, and sighed deeply.

She must put aside all thoughts of the earl. Nothing could come of them. She must forget the curly black hair she longed to touch and the deep blue eyes that sparkled with humor. She would not think of the way he had often taken her arm to assist her from the carriage, or how he had caught her up in his arms as if she'd weighed no more than a feather to carry her safely over a snowdrift last winter. The earl was married, and her dreams were improper. She would do better to dream of the unknown suitor who wrote such lovely words to her.

Vanessa reached the open door of the breakfast room and entered the sunny chamber. Its mullioned windows looked out over the inner courtyard where, even with winter fast approaching, flowers bloomed in profusion. Golden chrysanthemums lifted their shaggy heads to soak up the sun and purple asters bordered a variety of maples dressed in autumn's red and gold and several poplars sported golden leaves. In the center of the courtyard, a lofty pine rose up to the roofline, its branches heavy with giant pinecones. When they fell down to the courtyard, Vanessa and Millie would collect them and dip them in scented wax. After they had dried, they would be stored in baskets, one at each hearth, and used as aromatic fire starters.

Welles was as good as his word. The moment Vanessa had taken a chair, one of the footmen arrived with her chocolate. After he left, Vanessa retrieved the letter from her pocket and broke the seal.

The first words that met her eyes caused a rush of color to flood her cheeks, for the salutation read, *To my dearest love.*

Vanessa's color heightened as she read the words that compared her hair to shining gold spun from the sun and her eyes to an exotic emerald sea. He praised her figure, declaring her form should be captured in marble for all to admire, and the color of her lips, which he compared to wild strawberries. He complimented the graceful manner in which she carried herself, and even praised her trim ankle and the graceful arch of her foot.

Vanessa looked down at her feet with a frown. She wore half boots of leather, sturdily cut and of a size more nearly approximating a man's than a woman's. She did have a graceful arch, but it would be quite impossible for anyone to tell unless she removed her boots. Had he seen her bare her feet? When, and under what circumstances? Or was he merely writing these words to satisfy some deep yearning within himself, not caring they did not describe her in the slightest?

A glance in the Venetian glass that hung opposite the table confirmed the latter suspicion. No one would compare her hair to the sun. It was far more yellow than golden. Though her eyes were indeed green, no one, not even her loving papa, had ever compared them to an emerald sea.

Her chin was a bit too firm, her nose slightly off-center

in her face, her eyes too large and widely spaced. As far as capturing her figure in marble, it would take a veritable giant of a man to sculpt her form in a block of stone that massive and heavy. Her carriage, while proud, did not approximate grace, and her ankle was not trim, but sturdy.

She looked back down at the letter, and laughed. There were so many discrepancies she wondered whether the writer had ever made her acquaintance. If he had, he must be blind to have described her so inaccurately.

Perhaps he *was* blind? Vanessa considered the notion and then discarded it. A blind man could not write in such an even and careful hand. But he professed to love her, and Papa often said love was blind. Perhaps that was it. Her secret admirer did not see her as she was, but rather as he would prefer her to be.

Vanessa reached up to draw out the gold chain she wore beneath her plain but serviceable gown. Her secret admirer had sent her a small package on Valentine's Day two years ago. It had contained this lovely gold chain, and he'd asked her to wear it to remind her of him. It was highly improper for an unmarried miss to accept such an expensive gift, but she could not return it. She did not know his identity. Since the proper option had been closed to her, Vanessa had decided to wear it. There was no denying she had thought of him.

Last year, again on Valentine's Day, another gift arrived for her—a small gold heart, a tightly furled rosebud in its center, to hang from the gold chain. Thinking it the loveliest pendant she had ever seen, Vanessa had attached it to the chain and worn it faithfully for the past nine months. Though she had tried not to speculate, she found herself wondering, in odd moments, what her secret admirer would send her next Valentine's Day.

His letters and gifts had changed Vanessa's outlook on life. Instead of despairing that any young man might find her desirable, she had the assurance at least one gentleman found her attractive. He could be an aged widower, a young man barely out of the schoolroom, or the most unsuitable ruffian ever to walk Albion's shores. Someone found her desirable as a woman, and that was all that mattered.

At the sound of approaching footsteps, Vanessa hurriedly folded her letter and stuffed it back into her pocket. She had not told Millie of her secret admirer, choosing to keep the delicious and intriguing mystery to herself. She was just taking a sip of her morning chocolate when Millie burst into the room.

"Vanessa! I'm so glad you're back!"

"Gracious, you'd think I'd been gone a fortnight." Vanessa smiled at her young charge. Millie looked lovely this morning, dressed in a pale blue muslin gown that set off her blue-gray eyes. Her long brown hair was caught up in a ribbon, and her cheeks were becomingly pink. She was a far cry from the thin, silent waif Vanessa had encountered on her first day at Bridgeford Hall, but she still appeared more like a child than a young lady soon to celebrate her twentieth birthday.

"Did you bring your papa's book?" Millie's eyes shone with excitement.

"Of course. I perused it last night, and there are four more drawings to complete."

"Then we'd best get started." Millie picked up the bell and rang for one of the footmen, ordering a large breakfast for Vanessa and an equally hearty repast for herself. As the footman was about to leave, Millie stopped him. "Don't forget my surprise, George. Cook has set them out on a tray in the kitchen."

"Surprise?"

"Yes, I made something for you while you were gone."

"You did?" Vanessa smiled and raised her brows. "What is it, dear?"

Millie giggled and shook her head. "You will see in a

moment. I will only divulge that it is something to eat, something you favor very well indeed."

"Let me see." Vanessa pretended to ponder the subject for a moment. "Do not tell me you helped Cook make currant jam."

"No, you will like this far better than currant jam."

"I have it, then. It simply must be honey cakes."

Millie laughed. "You are wrong again. Try one more time."

"I do wish it would be . . ." Vanessa stopped and sighed. "Of course, that is merely wishful thinking."

"*What* is wishful thinking?" Millie leaned forward expectantly.

"Apple tartlets. I have been dreaming of apple tartlets for weeks on end. But I am certain whatever you made will please me every bit as much."

"Yes, indeed. I am certain it will." Millie dissolved in gales of laughter. "Close your eyes, Vanessa. Here is George with the tray."

Vanessa obediently shut her eyes as George set the tray on the table. Then, when Millie gave her permission to open her eyes, she gasped in pretended amazement. "Apple tartlets? Why, Millie, this is the best surprise!"

"You did not suspect?" Millie looked uncertain. "I could not help but laugh when you mentioned them, and I feared I had given all away."

"Not for a moment. I had no idea you would know how to make my favorite apple tartlets."

"Good." Millie leaned back, satisfied with the response. "They are slightly burned on the bottom. Cook said I used a bit too much honey and that is why they are so brown. Do you mind, Vanessa?"

"Not in the slightest. My mama always used a bit too much honey, and these are precisely the same as hers. Thank you. This is the nicest surprise I have ever had.

Shall we save one for your brother so he can enjoy them, too?"

"Stephen is back?" Millie's eyes widened when Vanessa nodded, and a wide happy smile spread over her face. "How wonderful! Stephen is here and you are here. Now my whole family is home!"

After they finished breakfast and went back to their chambers to don their walking dresses, Vanessa thought about what Millie had said. Millie considered her brother and Vanessa to be her whole family. It was a pity she did not remember her mother and father well, though it was not surprising. Millie had been a sickly child, and her parents had left her in the care of her nurse and her governess. The earl and the countess had made brief visits to the nursery and the schoolroom, but from what Vanessa had learned by speaking to the servants, their visits had been infrequent.

For all practical purposes, Millie had lived the life of an only child. Stephen, who was ten years Millie's senior, had gone off to school before she set foot outside the nursery. The village children had not been permitted to play with Millie, but the nurse thought her health too delicate, and it was no surprise Millie had failed to develop the necessary social skills. She had been taught to be polite, of course, and to comport herself as a lady should, but she didn't know how to get on with others her age.

Vanessa smiled, taking pleasure in comparing the desolate, isolated young woman she had first met with the effervescent and friendly young miss Millie had become. She had promised Stephen she would bring Millie out of her exile, and she was well on her way to achieving that goal. Her promise had been solemnly given three years and three months ago, a day that would live forever in her memory.

Now, waiting for Millie on the heavy wooden settle near the front entrance, Vanessa leaned back and thought about the day Stephen had hired her as Millie's companion. . . .

Three

The shadows were beginning to lengthen when Vanessa hopped down from the smart new carriage Becka Greene's husband had purchased for her as a bridal gift. They had gone to see Winifred Pearson's firstborn son, and both Vanessa and Becka had pronounced him adorable.

Winnie's husband, George, had beamed proudly as Winnie lifted the babe from his cradle and placed him carefully in Vanessa's arms. "You look fine with a babe in your arms, Vanessa," he'd said. "You'd best not wait much longer to have one of your own."

Vanessa had mulled over that remark ever since they had taken leave of Winnie and her husband. She was certain George had not meant to be unkind, but he had always spoken first and only later considered the effect of his words. She might have passed it off as another of George's unfortunate gaffes if both Winnie and Becka had not glared at him and quickly changed the subject to a discussion of the church's autumn festival.

"I hope you're not overset at the remark George made." Becka turned to Vanessa with an anxious expression. "I am certain he only meant you looked quite charming with a child in your arms."

Vanessa laughed. "It is useless to attempt to wrap it in clean linen, Becka. We both know precisely what George meant. If I do not marry soon, I will have little chance of having children of my own."

"But you are not so old as all that." Becka's anxious smile did not quite reach her eyes. "Many women prefer to wait until they are more mature to marry."

Vanessa sighed, smiling at her younger friend. "I am just turned twenty-three, Becka, and I have never had a suitor. If I am to have children, I must first find a man to marry me."

"Yes, there is that." Becka looked thoughtful. "Have you made the acquaintance of my brother-in-law? He is a widower and quite personable for a man of his years."

Vanessa could not stop the bubble of mirth that rose in her throat. She covered it quickly with a cough, and managed to nod. "Indeed I have, Becka. Parson Greene is a most admirable man. But I do not think he is seeking a wife."

"Oh, but he is! In his last letter to us, he remarked his duties as parson would be much less difficult with a wife at his side. And the parsonage at Charsborough is not so far that you could not visit your papa."

Vanessa nodded, stifling her urge to laugh at the thought of wedding Parson Greene. He was ten years older than Papa, a full two heads shorter than she, and as stern and uncompromising as the cliffs that rose in sheer vertical walls by the coast of Dover.

"If you like, I could arrange a small dinner party so you could further your acquaintance with him." Becka sounded hopeful. "He is occupied with his parish work during the week, but perhaps he could come to us on a Friday. We could enjoy a nice family dinner and listen to him read in the evening."

Vanessa grimaced. Parson Greene had a thin reedy voice pitched higher than usual for a man. He sounded rather like a crow when he spoke and he had stated, during their initial meeting at Becka and Robert's wedding, that the only reading materials he perused were religious treatises.

"Shall I attempt it, Vanessa?" A fleeting expression of panic crossed Becka's pretty face. "Parson Greene would be required to spend the night with us, as it is a journey of two hours from Charsborough, but I am certain Robert would agree."

Vanessa burst into laughter. "You are a true martyr to offer your hospitality when you know full well Robert cannot abide his brother."

"But Robert thinks so highly of you. And though he often disagrees with his brother, I am certain he would go to any lengths to . . ."

"No, Becka." Vanessa interrupted her friend. "I am not so desperate as that. To be completely truthful, I must admit I share Robert's opinion of his brother. Parson Greene is horribly stuffy, and I should far rather marry a . . . a billy goat!"

Becka stared and then began to giggle. "I should be telling a bouncer if I did not agree completely. But I can think of no one else. There are simply no unmarried men left in Bridgeford Village."

"Do not be anxious on my account. Someone will come along. If not, I shall content myself with playing auntie to your children."

Becka's cheeks colored slightly. "But we have no children."

"You will, never fear." Vanessa grinned. "I have seen the loving glances pass between the two of you, and it is only a matter of time. Do not forget, you have been married less than six months."

Becka's cheeks turned even rosier. "Yes, that is true. Perhaps . . . it *is* possible that . . . but I must not tempt the Fates by putting it into words."

"How wonderful, Becka!" Vanessa reached up to hug

her friend. "You may rest assured I will not breathe a word of it until you are certain."

Though Becka's cheeks were high with color, her lips turned up in a happy smile. "I will hold you to your word, Vanessa, for I have not even confided in Robert. I should not like to disappoint him if I am mistaken."

"Of course." Vanessa nodded. "Do not forget to drink warm milk in lieu of tea. Papa believes milk is essential to the growth of healthy bones. He also believes green vegetables are important for a baby's development, and fresh meat for the stamina of a mother. Have you felt at all peckish in the mornings?"

"No. But this very morning when Daisy brought in Robert's rasher of bacon, I discovered I could not abide the aroma."

"Perfect!" Vanessa started to grin. "If the same occurs again tomorrow morning, I should think you are indeed increasing. You will come to tell me, won't you, Becka?"

Becka nodded quickly. "I will. But should I be riding in my carriage if what I suspect is true?"

"It will do you no harm, so long as you tell your driver to proceed slowly. Papa is fond of saying nature's cushion for a babe is perfectly designed. You need only use your good sense and avoid things that are too strenuous, like galloping on horseback and jouncing about on rough roads for hours upon end. You should take leisurely walks, make certain you enjoy a full night's sleep, and avoid gowns that are tightly fitted and restraining."

"Thank you, Vanessa." Becka nodded. "I will do everything you say."

After a final hug good-bye, Becka's driver set the team in motion and Vanessa walked up the path to the cottage she shared with her father. She called out when she opened the door, but there was no answer.

Vanessa went quickly to her chamber to remove her best gown and hang it in her clothespress. She changed to a serviceable muslin that had seen better years, released her unruly curls from the tight knot at the back of her neck, and smiled in relief as she pulled on her most comfortable slippers. After brushing and then capturing the cloud of curls sprang out in every direction, she wrapped a loose ribbon around her hair and let it fall where it would.

Staring at her reflection in the glass hung over her dressing table, Vanessa smiled. Had Becka actually thought she would welcome the attentions of Parson Greene? Such an unlikely match would be too absurd for words.

Shrugging, Vanessa turned from the glass and hurried down the staircase. She could scarcely wait to tell Papa what Becka had suggested. She would put on the teakettle, prepare a cold supper, and they would enjoy a laugh together over the thought of her as Parson Greene's proper wife.

As she neared her father's study, Vanessa heard his voice raised in a question. He was answered by a deeper male voice, and Vanessa realized he was closeted with a visitor. Since her father had not taken his visitor to the chamber he used as his apothecary shop, Vanessa assumed his guest was a colleague or friend.

As she passed the partially open door, Vanessa glanced in. The sight that greeted her eyes made her stop in midstep and return to the doorway for a second look. The man seated before her father's desk was extremely tall, with broad shoulders. Though she was only able to view his back, Vanessa noted he had a full head of dark curly hair, worn slightly longer than was usual. His arms appeared as sturdy as the branches of a massive oak. His voice was deep and forceful. Though not intending to eavesdrop, Vanessa heard his words.

"You simply must help me, Mr. Holland. The situation

is most untenable. When I returned, I learned my sister had not spoken to a soul in days."

"Not even the servants?"

"No." The man shook his head. "Her abigail reports she simply nods or shakes her head when she is queried. Though she has always been slight of build, she is losing flesh at an alarming rate."

"She would not speak even to you?"

"She greeted me, but it was an effort for her. And during our dinner last evening, she ate only enough to keep a sparrow alive. She seems to have lost all interest in living, and I do not know how to help her."

"You say her governess has retired?"

"Yes, and also her nurse. The two ladies were cousins, you see, and well advanced in years. They expressed their desire to retire to Brighton, and I could not refuse them. They came to us when Millie was born and have stayed with her all these years."

"Then you wish to hire another governess and nurse to replace them?"

"No. Millie is uncommonly intelligent and I believe she has learned all a governess might teach her. Though she is frail, she does not require a nurse. A companion might serve her better, and is the reason I came to you. You are acquainted with all who live in Bridgeford Village. Could you recommend someone for the position?"

"Would you say your sister is attempting to withdraw from the world?" Vanessa frowned at her father's words, for he seldom sounded this anxious.

"Precisely!" The man gave a deep sigh. "She has never been in perfect health, you understand, but since the death of our parents, she has taken to spending every waking moment in her chambers. I do not believe she has ventured outside for the past six months."

"Has your sister no friends?"

"None. Millie has always been remarkably unsociable.

She is fast approaching her seventeenth year of seclusion, and I fear she is accustomed to being alone. I suspect she is too frightened to attempt to make the acquaintance of others her age."

Vanessa drew in her breath sharply, her heart going out to the frightened young miss and her concerned brother. Perhaps she should offer to introduce this slip of a girl to her own friends. Lord knew she had plenty, and they would treat this unfortunate soul kindly.

"When I married shortly after my parents' death, I hoped my wife might provide companionship for Millie." The man's voice was uncertain and filled with an emotion Vanessa could not identify. "But Phoebe took ill on our wedding trip, and the doctors advised me to settle her in warmer, sunnier climes until she recovered."

"From what does she suffer?"

"A lung ailment. She is much improved, but not yet ready to return to England. And this presents another problem, Mr. Holland. I am required to travel frequently, and Millie is too frail to join me. I do not wish to leave her behind with only the servants to care for her."

Vanessa frowned. She thought she knew every family in the area, but she could not fathom who this man might be. He spoke well and must be wealthy if he traveled so frequently.

"You must tell me precisely what type of companion you seek for your sister." Vanessa heard the scratch of a pen against vellum. Her father was indulging his passion for making lists. "We must catalogue the attributes you require."

There was silence before the stranger spoke. "She should be kind and generous in her attentions—I should think most important—not so old as to have forgotten the dreams of a young girl, be lively, cheerful, and above all, sociable so she may guide my sister in making friends."

"Good." Vanessa noted her father seemed pleased by

the man's words. "I assume she should also be intelligent."

"Yes, indeed. Millie is enamored of books. It would be useful if she could discuss them with a companion who was also well read, and it would please me greatly if my sister's companion also possessed an excellent sense of humor."

"A sense of humor?" Vanessa's father sounded puzzled.

"Yes. Now I think on it, I regard it as the most important attribute of all. Millie does not laugh at all, and I have seldom seen her smile. She has no concept of fun or whimsy and is far too solemn for her years. It would please me above all else if I could hear her laugh just once."

"I see." Her father's pen scratched again. "You must give me time to consider this. I cannot think of anyone who possesses every one of the attributes you desire. Perhaps if I peruse my list of acquaintances, I may find someone who . . ."

"Me, Papa!" Vanessa stepped through the doorway and strode into the chamber. "I am perfect for the position. Indeed, there is no one better."

Vanessa laughed at her father's shocked expression and then turned to address the man who had leaned forward in his chair. "I am Vanessa Holland, and I possess every one of those attributes. And you are?"

"Stephen Thurston." The man rose from his chair, and Vanessa's eyes widened in surprise. Not only was he was the tallest and most handsome man she had ever seen, he was the ninth Earl of Bridgeford.

"My lord." Vanessa dipped her head. "I would not have barged into the chamber if I had known my father was closeted with you."

The earl smiled at her and took her hand. "Then it is

fortunate you did *not* know, Miss Holland, for you seem to be perfect for the position."

"Yes. Vanessa *would* be perfect." Mr. Holland turned to his noble visitor. "My daughter is both lively and friendly, and she possesses a most impish sense of humor."

Vanessa smiled. "My father is too modest. I am also extremely well read and have never been accused of shrinking from a difficult task. I paint with watercolors, can perform with ease upon the pianoforte, and will sing when asked, though my voice has more volume than accuracy. I also know how to cook an acceptable meal, write a letter as rapidly as my father can dictate, and ride neck-or-nothing if the occasion warrants. Did I mention I speak four languages fluently and have been known to argue philosophy quite handily with several highly placed professors at Cambridge and Oxford?"

"That is quite enough, Vanessa." Though her father's voice was stern, the corners of his mouth were twitching. "The earl and I concede you are well qualified, but are you certain you wish to assume such a demanding position?"

Vanessa nodded quickly. "It would not be in the least demanding, Papa, and you may rest assured I am the very one to bring Millie out of her exile. I am certain to make her laugh. How many times have you told me, Papa, one would have to be blind, deaf, and dumb not to laugh at one of my outrageous comments?"

"Too many times to count, my dear." Mr. Holland turned to the earl. "Vanessa possesses another attribute you did not think to add to your list. She has assisted me in treating many ailments, and she will know precisely how to proceed if your sister takes ill. This should be of great comfort while you are away."

The earl nodded. "You need not attempt to convince

me, Mr. Holland. I daresay Miss Holland is even more perfect than I could have wished."

"Then I am hired, my lord?" Vanessa flashed him a grin.

The earl nodded. "Indeed you are, Miss Holland."

"Vanessa. You must call me Vanessa, my lord. It will make me appear to be more of an age with your sister, and I should like her to think of me as a friend."

"Vanessa." The earl repeated her name. "And you must call me Stephen, precisely as Millie does."

Vanessa raised her brows, pondered the concept for a moment, and then nodded. "Yes. I take your point. It would seem quite odd if I *my lorded* you and you *Vanessaed* me. Poor Millie would be hopelessly confused as to our relationship."

The earl threw back his head to laugh, and Vanessa thought again how very handsome he was. Then he sobered and turned to her father. "We must now discuss your daughter's salary, Mr. Holland."

"Oh, you need not pay me." Vanessa laughed. "Simply supply me with food. Papa often says he fears I shall eat him out of house and home."

The earl stared at her for a moment and then chuckled. "I do believe I can manage a bit more than food. You shall receive a generous stipend and a suite of rooms close to Millie. In addition, I will provide you with a new wardrobe, and . . ."

"But I do not require a new wardrobe." Vanessa frowned. "Do not judge me by this poor excuse for a gown. I assure you I have others."

The earl shook his head. "I was not criticizing your appearance, Vanessa. I should like Millie to have a new wardrobe, and she will regard the whole process as less of an ordeal if you are also to be pricked and prodded and measured."

"If that is your only intention, I shall accept a new wardrobe with gratitude. But in addition to our new gowns, may I have leave to commission a riding habit and two walking dresses each?"

"Anything you wish. But there is no need to order a riding habit for Millie. She has never learned to ride."

At this revelation, Vanessa regarded the earl with some concern. "Does Millie fear horses?"

"I do not think so. She always expressed a keen interest when she saw me riding from her window. But her nurse and her governess said she was too delicate to ride."

"I see." Vanessa raised her brows. "And did either of those two ladies ride?"

"Millie's nurse did not. I remember quite well. The poor woman was terrified of horses. Now I consider it, I do not believe Millie's governess rode, either."

"Perhaps it was not Millie who was disinclined to learn to ride." Vanessa took in his startled expression and drove her point home. "It is even possible your sister was not as delicate as those two ladies led you to believe."

The earl frowned slightly. "But what reason would they have to deceive me?"

"It may be similar to the case of the doctor who desires to purchase a new carriage." Mr. Holland spoke up. "He knows if his services are no longer required, he will forfeit his patients' fees. Is there any doubt the ladies in question benefited from their tenure at Bridgeford Hall?"

The earl shook his head. "No, indeed. They were well reimbursed for their services."

"Precisely." Mr. Holland nodded. "And at what age does a healthy child no longer require the services of a nurse?"

"Why . . . I am not certain. But I would assume few nurses retain their positions once a governess is hired."

"And a governess would no longer be required when

the young lady goes off to a suitable academy," Vanessa said. "Is that not correct?"

"Yes, I assume so. But Millie was far too frail to attend a . . ." The earl stopped speaking and a frown crossed his face. "It's clear you suspect Millie's nurse and governess of exaggerating her condition so they could maintain their employment. That may have been true, but there is no denying Millie is frail at the present time."

"Let us see whether Millie's condition improves in a month's time. If it does not, then Papa and I will admit we were wrong."

"Are you proposing a wager?" The earl smiled.

"Indeed, I am. If Millie is not improved in both health and spirits after the first month of my care, I will forfeit my salary for a full year."

"You are certain?"

"I am," Vanessa stated. "Do we have a wager, sir?"

The earl laughed. "Not quite yet. You have not named the prize I must forfeit in the event you win. Would an extra year's salary satisfy you?"

Vanessa stared at him in utter shock. "No, indeed not! I could not accept a year's salary for duties I did not perform."

"A piece of fine jewelry then? Or the horse of your choice from my stables?"

"No. Those stakes are far too high." Vanessa smiled. "Books. I should like books if I win. If you will agree to allow me to read any volume in your library, we shall consider it done."

"It is a wager then, but I shall sweeten the pot," the earl said. "You may order any volumes you wish from Lackington's Bookshop in London for the entire tenure of your position as my sister's companion."

"Are you so very rich, then? You had best be as wealthy

as Golden Ball, for I must warn you there are hundreds of books I should like to own."

"I promise you may have every one of them and more, so long as you can perform the miracle of turning Millie into a happy, healthy young lady."

"It is done, sir!" Vanessa shook his hand and turned to her father. "You had best think of where to build shelves for my library, Papa, for I am determined to win this wager."

Four

The sound of running footsteps jolted Vanessa from her memories and she smiled when Millie arrived at her side, dressed in one of the gowns Vanessa had ordered specifically for walking through the woods.

The creation was Vanessa's own design, made of cherry red muslin. The skirt was half the fullness of an ordinary gown and the hemline at least five inches shorter than the modiste had deemed proper. Indeed, Madame LaTeure had been scandalized at the suggestion the skirt should end at midcalf, refusing to consider Vanessa's explanation that a longer skirt would impede their progress when they walked through the woods.

Vanessa had bowed to her wishes, agreeing Madame should fashion the dress at the length she deemed proper. When the walking dresses had been completed and Madame LaTeure had taken her leave, Vanessa cut off the extra material and hemmed their dresses to the length she had originally desired.

"These stockings are a lark, Vanessa." Millie giggled as she glanced down at her bright red and yellow clockwork stockings made of heavy cambric.

Vanessa nodded in agreement, smiling down at her own orange and bright purple stockings. "I admit they are highly unusual, but stockings like these have saved me from many a painful scratch. And dressed in our bright clothing and colorful stockings, no hunter shall mistake us for game."

"I brought your hat, Vanessa." Millie handed her a straw chip bonnet dyed a bright orange. She donned her own, a similar design in red, and tied the ribbons beneath her chin. "Where do we venture today?"

Vanessa picked up one of the heavy baskets that contained their painting supplies and handed the other to Millie. "We will start with the oak grove. I must draw pilewort and its roots."

"Pilewort?" Millie raised her brows. "I have never heard mention of it before. What ailment does it cure?"

"You do not wish to know, but if you think about its name for a moment, you may very well guess." Vanessa smiled, remembering the section of her father's book dealt with the relief of hemorrhoids.

Mille's eyes widened as she hit upon the answer, and she blushed in embarrassment. "You are quite right. I did not wish to know. What other drawings shall we render?"

"Stavesacre, anise, and common ivy. There is ivy in the oak grove. While I sketch the pilewort, you may complete the ivy."

Millie nodded and they set off on their jaunt, both young ladies taking pleasure in the sunny morning. Vanessa led the way to the oak grove at a brisk pace, sweeping low branches out of the way with her stick. After a quarter hour of exertion, they arrived at the spot Vanessa had chosen.

"Was my pace too tiring?" Vanessa turned to Millie, whose color was high in her cheeks.

"Not in the slightest. I am not at all out of breath and I find my stamina is almost as great as yours."

"That is but one of the benefits of regular exercise." Vanessa gestured toward a bed of ivy near one of the massive oaks. "There is your subject, Millie. Choose several well-shaped leaves and sketch them. Papa said if your drawing is as fine as the one you made of the spring violets, he will use it in his book."

Millie's lips parted in surprise. "Your father will use *my* drawing?"

"Yes, indeed. It is to be placed in a section concerning the use of medicinal flora by ancient armies, so your drawing must be perfectly accurate."

"I promise you it will be." Millie looked very determined as she walked to the bed of ivy and searched for the perfect specimen. "Whatever does ivy have to do with armies?"

"Papa found a reference to it in a military history written over two centuries ago. The leaves of the ivy are useful in treating corns and calluses caused by ill-fitting footwear."

Millie was clearly intrigued by this notion. "How did they use it?"

"The instructions are to take two ivy leaves and soak them in vinegar for a full day and night. One is applied to the corn or the callus until its virtue has been extracted; then the other is applied. When it has dried, the corn or callus may be removed with no pain."

"Does it work?" Millie raised her brows.

"Indeed, yes. Papa made use of it with several of his patients and found it a very good remedy."

"Should we gather some ivy leaves for Cook? She is forever complaining about her bunions. Perhaps the remedy would serve for those, as well."

"We shall ask Papa when he comes for tea. No doubt he will wish to examine her feet before he proposes a treatment. And that puts me in mind of another bit of news I have for you. Papa is bringing a friend with him."

"How wonderful!" Millie smiled happily. "I do hope it is that nice older gentleman from Cambridge. I found him most charming."

"No, Millie, not Professor Ewing. Papa is bringing the

rector's daughter, Prudence Hawthorne. She is only one year older than you are and has been wishing to make your acquaintance."

Millie was silent for a long moment. Then she sighed. "You know how shy I become with others my age. I never know what to say, and I am hopelessly tongue-tied. I do not suppose you would excuse me from tea?"

"No." Vanessa put down her trowel and took Millie's hand. "Prudence needs your assistance with the Christmas celebration she is planning for the children of the village."

Millie appeared dumbfounded. "*My* assistance? But I know nothing about planning a celebration. I have never attended such a celebration, much less planned one."

"Calm yourself, Millie, and I shall tell you how all this came about." Vanessa gave her a reassuring smile. "When I mentioned the clever little animals you fashion from bits of cloth, Prudence remarked they would be perfect for the celebration she has planned. She begged me to introduce her so she could ask if you will teach her how to make them."

Millie looked relieved. "And that is all she wishes from me?"

"Yes, dear. Perhaps you could fashion one for her at tea this very afternoon so she can observe your method. You would not mind teaching her, would you?"

"Of course not." Millie began to smile. "I would be delighted."

Vanessa turned away to hide her pleased expression. Millie had reacted precisely as she had thought. Now that there was a stated purpose for her meeting with Prudence, she was no longer anxious over making her acquaintance. It would also give the two young ladies a topic for discourse, one Millie knew in advance.

"Which animal should I teach her to make?" Millie

placed two ivy leaves on a piece of white muslin and prepared to sketch them.

"The most simple, I should think. If you begin with the easiest, Prudence will gain confidence in her ability to make them."

"Of course. I should have thought of that. I will begin with the bear, then, as it has only five parts."

"Five?" Vanessa raised her brows. "I count eight. There are four legs, a body, a head, and two ears."

Millie giggled. "No, Vanessa. That is the way I was used to make them, but I have come up with a simpler method. The body, head, and ears are all of one piece."

"How is this possible?"

"They are simply twisted and tied off very tightly with thread. It saves much time to do them way. Then all one has to do is sew on the legs and paint the features of the face."

"That is very clever, indeed. You must show Prudence one of every animal you have made so she may see how many there are."

Millie's eyes began to sparkle. "Do you think she would mind visiting my chambers? It would be easier than carrying them all down to the drawing room."

"I am certain she would not mind at all." Vanessa busied herself with her sketchbook. Millie had never offered to show her collection of creations to any visitor before. It gave her hope that Prudence could persuade Millie to take an active part in the children's Christmas celebration. That would mean Vanessa had succeeded in drawing her shy charge completely out of her shell.

"Oh, how charming!" Prudence laughed in delight as Millie presented her with the animal she had named Cubbie. "A real bear cub could never be so darling as this, and it certainly would not be content to be cradled in a child's arms. You simply must teach me how to make them, Millie. I daresay little Susie Yardley should love to receive a Cubbie for her Christmas gift. She is just turned two years of age and this would be perfect for her."

Millie grinned proudly and Vanessa noticed she was not a bit shy when she was engaged in discussing her creations. "It was really quite simple to make, Prudence, and I will show you precisely how to go about it. Is this child a relative of yours?"

"No. Her mother and father do not have the funds to buy toys for their children. I should like to make one for Susie and something for the other children, as well."

"How kind of you!" Millie nodded quickly. "Perhaps I could help. How old are the other children?"

"There is the baby, and then Susie. And then there are the twins, Kenneth and Paul, who are four years of age."

Millie smiled. "A soft rattle should do nicely for the baby, and I would think Lionel would be perfect for the boys."

"Lionel?" Prudence began to grin. "No doubt Lionel is a lion. Am I right?"

Mr. Holland nodded. "You are, my dear. Millie's lions are large and loosely stuffed, and they serve quite admirably as bed pillows. They are my favorite of her animals."

"Mine are the frogs," Vanessa spoke up. "Millie made me a present of one for my birthday last year and she named it Ferguson. I would think a Ferguson should be perfect for Tommy Wilks."

Prudence nodded. "Indeed, it would be. Tommy Wilks is thoroughly enamored of frogs."

"How many of my creatures would you like to learn to make?" Millie looked a bit puzzled.

"All of them." Prudence sighed softly. "I must make forty toys for the children of the village before the Christmas celebration."

Millie raised her brows. "Forty? You must give one to every child, then."

"Yes. You see, Millie, many parents in the village cannot buy Christmas presents for their children. Many have all they can do to keep food upon the table and a roof over their family's head. Toys are a luxury they can ill afford."

"Then we must help them. No child should go without a toy at Christmas. Let us go to my chambers, Prudence, and I will show you the animals I have made. When we return, we shall make a list of the village children and their ages and decide which toys will best suit them."

Vanessa grinned at her father as Millie and Prudence left the drawing room. Their voices floated back as they hurried up the staircase, two young ladies enjoying an easy camaraderie.

"I do believe you have done it, my dear." Mr. Holland returned his daughter's grin. "Millie did not appear to be at all shy with Prudence."

"You are quite right, Papa. It is all I could have hoped for."

Mr. Holland took another pastry from the tea tray. "But you must have another goal in mind."

"You are quite correct, Papa. I hope Millie will become even more involved in the children's Christmas celebration."

"You should like her to attend the affair?"

Vanessa nodded, reaching out to pour her father another cup of tea. "I am relying upon Prudence's ability to convince her not only to attend, but to pass out the presents."

Father and daughter sat in companionable silence for a moment and then Vanessa produced the drawing Millie had done very morning. "Do you think this will serve for the illustration of the ivy, Papa?"

"Very well, indeed. You have taught Millie well."

"Oh, she did not need much instruction. Her governess did *some* things right. She taught Millie to sketch accurately, and her embroidery is truly lovely."

"It is little wonder, for with the exception of reading, it is all she was permitted to do."

"I know, Papa." Vanessa sighed. "And for my first full year as Millie's companion, the poor dear shuddered at the thought of picking up a sketchbook or a needle. I do think we are well over that hurdle. Now she delights in sketching, so long as she is given leave to sketch outside the confines of her chambers."

Mr. Holland smiled. "But she no longer embroiders."

"No, of course she does not. She did not care to follow a pattern not of her making, and I do not see why she should. Now she sews animals of her own design and delights in her charming creations. Truly, all Millie needed was a nudge in the right direction. I have not done so much for her as Stephen would have me believe."

There was the sound of girlish laughter in the distance, and Mr. Holland favored his daughter with a wink. "You have not? I seem to recall Millie was well on her way to becoming a recluse before you arrived. And Stephen himself said she never laughed."

"Yes, is true. But truly, Papa, I . . ."

Mr. Holland held up his hand for silence, interrupting Vanessa's further denials. "Listen for yourself, daughter, and acknowledge the miracle you have wrought. I am uncommonly proud of you."

"Thank you, Papa." Vanessa gave him a smile. "Just listen to Millie. It sounds as if she's running down the staircase."

A moment later, Prudence walked into the drawing room. She was grinning widely as she took her chair once again.

"What is it, Prudence?" Vanessa turned to her friend.

"Millie." Prudence laughed. "I do declare, she is all you have said and more. And you never mentioned she was so generous."

Mr. Holland nodded. "We heard her offer to help you make the toy animals."

"It is not just that." Prudence smiled happily. "Millie asked if I should like her assistance in planning the party and helping with the decorations."

Vanessa nodded. "I had hoped she might. Where is she now, Prudence?"

"I am not certain. When I told her the celebration would be held in father's church, she asked whether all in the village would be invited. I replied they would, but we schedule families to come at specific times, as the church is too small to hold everyone. That was when she said she must speak with her brother on a matter of some urgency, and asked me to wait for her here."

Vanessa frowned. "That is strange, indeed. Did Millie say why she needed to speak to the earl?"

"No."

Before Vanessa had time to digest this puzzling piece of news, one of the earl's liveried footmen entered the drawing room and crossed the floor to stand before her. He bowed slightly and handed her a sheet of folded vellum. "M'lord said to give this to you, Miss Vanessa."

"Thank you, Harold." Vanessa opened the sheet, scanned it, and nodded to the footman. "Please tell him we shall be along shortly."

When the footman had taken his leave, Prudence turned to Vanessa anxiously. "You look uncommonly pleased, Vanessa. What is it?"

"A summons from the earl." Vanessa looked down at the paper once again. "He requests our presence in his study."

"For what purpose?" Mr. Holland smiled as he noticed his daughter's shining eyes.

"So we may assist Millie in planning the Christmas feast and celebration for the entire village that is to take place at Bridgeford Hall."

Five

"We should revive the custom." Stephen smiled at Millie, who sat next to him at the long oak table near the windows. "I remember the last celebration, though I could not have been older than four or five. My nurse let me visit the playroom, where the village children were free to enjoy their own entertainments."

"They were not allowed to join their parents?" Mr. Holland looked perplexed.

"Indeed they were, for the initial part of the celebration." Millie hastened to correct this erroneous impression. "But Stephen has found my grandmother's account of the annual affair in her journals. The youngest of the children soon grew tired of the festivities and wished to be at home in their beds. She filled the second-largest chamber with cots and cradles for the youngest children and staffed it with a group of nannies hired especially for the occasion."

Stephen nodded. "My grandmother also turned the largest chamber into a playroom for the older children, who were not interested in watching their parents dance. A stage was fashioned at the far end of the room. When I peeked in, they had just finished viewing a puppet show and were about to be entertained by a magician."

Prudence smiled at the earl. "How thoughtful of the countess! The mothers were free to enjoy the dancing without concerning themselves over the care of their children. It must have been a marvelous evening for them."

"By my grandmother's account, it was." Stephen nodded. "According to her records, the dancing went on until the sky began to lighten on Christmas Day."

"Could we do the same for our Christmas celebration?" Millie glanced at her brother with shining eyes.

"We shall. But there is much to be accomplished in the next six weeks to organize such an affair. Do you think you and Miss Hawthorne will be able to accomplish the arrangements in such a short time?"

"I am certain we can." Millie beamed at him, then turned to Vanessa. "You will help us, won't you, Vanessa?"

"Yes, and I daresay Papa will, also. But your brother is quite correct in cautioning us there is little time to waste. Shall we leave him to his work and discuss this further amongst ourselves?"

"Yes." Millie was smiling happily as she rose to her feet. "We must first make a list of what is to be done. I shall ring for more tea in the drawing room and we will begin immediately."

Vanessa was about to follow them from the chamber when Stephen took her arm. "Would you stay a moment? There is an important matter I should like to discuss with you."

"Of course." Vanessa made her excuses to her father, Millie, and Prudence.

After the door had closed behind the excited trio, Stephen led her to a pair of comfortable leather chairs pulled up next to the hearth. "Please be seated, Vanessa, and I shall pour you a bit of sherry."

Vanessa sank into one of the massive, overstuffed chairs. It cradled her like a pair of soft arms, and she sighed in satisfaction. "What is it, Stephen? Are you entertaining second thoughts about this huge undertaking?"

"No, indeed." Stephen handed her a glass of sherry,

poured a bit of brandy for himself, and sat down in the other chair. "I merely wish to offer my congratulations."

"On what?"

Stephen laughed and took her hand. "If you had promised me three years ago Millie would ask permission to host a party for the entire village at Bridgeford Hall, I would have accused you of wishful thinking. But she has, and it is time to reward you for your efforts on Millie's behalf. I will draft a letter this very afternoon to set up an account in your name at Lackington's Bookshop. You may order any volumes you please, Vanessa, and the bills will be sent to me. It is little enough payment for returning my sister's happiness to her."

"Thank you, Stephen, but I think it a bit premature." Vanessa felt a blush rise to her cheeks at the warm feelings his touch evoked. "I had hoped Millie might begin with something a bit smaller than a celebration for the entire village."

"Then you are not certain she shall succeed in this endeavor?"

Vanessa shook her head. "Oh, she will succeed, never fear. Prudence, Papa, and I shall make certain of that. But I do not know whether Millie will feel *comfortable* in the society of others. That she is so eager to host this celebration gives me a great deal of hope, but we must wait and see her reaction to others of her age."

"Yes, there is that." Stephen gave Vanessa's hand a pat and released it. "But if she does seem comfortable, do you think we dare risk planning her London debut?"

"For this coming Season?" Vanessa laced her fingers together, sorely missing the touch of his hand on hers.

"She is nearly twenty years of age, Vanessa, and most young ladies of her standing have already made their bows to society. If we wait much longer, the traditional avenues will be closed to Millie and there will be a great deal of speculation as to why she was not presented earlier."

"Yes, I suppose so." Vanessa sighed deeply. "But I am not certain she is ready. Perhaps we could look upon the Christmas celebration as a test of her social skills and observe her carefully to make certain she is no longer so shy and frightened."

Stephen nodded, standing up to indicate their interview was at an end. "You are quite right, Vanessa. Let us meet midway through the celebration and compare our observations. If we both judge Millie ready to enjoy her first Season in London, I shall be delighted to set the wheels in motion."

The day before the celebration, Vanessa grinned as Millie wrapped a folded silk scarf around her head and tied it in the back. "Is it truly necessary for me to be blindfolded? I could simply shut my eyes and promise not to peek."

"Do not be taken in by her, Millie." Prudence's voice was filled with laughter. "I have known Vanessa all my life, and she is far too curious not to peek."

Mr. Holland chuckled, seizing Vanessa's left arm. "Right you are, Prudence. Lean on me, daughter, and I will steady you. Millie, take her other arm and we will lead her inside the ballroom."

Vanessa gave way to the inevitable. For the past four days, Millie, Prudence, and her papa had secreted themselves in the ballroom, directing the workmen who were to accomplish the decorations they had designed. She had not been allowed to view the proceedings, as the three conspirators had decided it should be a surprise. Instead, Vanessa had interviewed nannies, choosing which ladies should be employed to care for the village children.

Stephen had gone off to London to engage the entertainers. He was expected to return this afternoon with the jugglers, magicians, puppeteers, and musicians he had hired. Their quarters were ready and waiting. Before he left, he had given orders to a team of local carpenters, who had built wooden cots upon which tick mattresses could be placed. His troop of entertainers was to be housed in the large loft above the stables, and all was in readiness for their arrival.

Vanessa had seen to the accommodations for the nannies, and a half dozen small bedchambers with two beds in each had been made ready for the ladies she had engaged. She was more than pleased at the response to her inquiries, and she had hired a dozen excellent nannies. Several were related to families in the village, and Vanessa had engaged them on the spot, as they were previously acquainted with the children.

"Easy, daughter." Mr. Holland laughed as Vanessa attempted to step forward briskly. "There is a large object directly before you and we must make our way around it. We will step to the left."

Vanessa's nostrils flared slightly at the delightful scent pervading the air. It reminded her of the forest. At first she could not place it, but then recognized the scent of pine boughs. "Are we almost there? I am anxious to see what wonders you have accomplished."

"Yes. One more step, Vanessa." Millie tugged her a bit further to the left. "Now you must sit, for we have placed a chair for you."

Vanessa felt the seat of the chair against the back of her legs and she lowered herself gently to its cushion. "I am seated. Please do not keep me in suspense any longer."

"Wait! I should like to see Vanessa's reaction for myself," a deep voice called out.

Vanessa smiled. Stephen was back from London. Footsteps approached, and she felt a deliciously solid hand against her back. With Stephen's presence, the surprise was complete.

"Remove the blindfold, Millie." Stephen's voice was filled with pride. "I am certain Vanessa will agree your decorations are superb."

The blindfold was whisked away and Vanessa gasped as the full wonder of the ballroom sparkled before her. "Why, this is the loveliest sight I have ever seen! You must give me a moment to look around so I may appreciate all you've done."

Vanessa smiled as she gazed around the huge ballroom. Garlands of pine branches and holly draped from the center of the largest chandelier to the sconces on all four walls, forming a fragrant bower under which to dance. Enormous bows fashioned of bright red velvet hung above every window; cushions of rich dark green velvet rested on every chair. The dais for the orchestra had been dressed with garlands and ribbons, and gardenias and deep red camellias from the earl's greenhouse colored the perimeter of the chamber, their pots wrapped with swatches of red and green velvet.

But the most amazing sight of all left Vanessa speechless for long moments. At the center of the ballroom stood a tall pine in an enormous dark green wooden tub.

"What do you think of our efforts, Vanessa?" Millie clasped her hands together, clearly pleased by her companion's stunned reaction.

"It is a miracle," Vanessa sighed in wonder. "However did you move large pine in here?"

"With great care," Mr. Holland said. "It took the gardener several days to choose it and several more to excavate the roots and replant it in the tub the carpenters built."

"It is a *Tannenbaum*, is it not?" Vanessa turned to the earl, who had mentioned the Germanic custom of moving a pine tree inside a dwelling and decorating it for Christmas.

"It is. And a diplomat friend kindly secured the decorations for us. He has just returned from Berlin."

"Oh, let us begin to decorate it immediately!" Millie clapped her hands in delight.

Stephen smiled at his sister's enthusiasm, but shook his head. "I think it best to wait until this evening, my dear."

"But why?"

Vanessa smiled up at the earl, immediately understanding his reason for the delay. "No doubt it would be better done when darkness has fallen so we may judge the decorations under the light of the chandeliers."

"Oh, of course," Millie said. "I did not think of that. Will we have candles on the branches?"

The earl nodded. "Yes, but my friend told me of an unfortunate fire that was caused by *Tannenbaum* candles only last year. Let us have the servants light them immediately before our guests are to enter the ballroom. After all have admired the sight, we shall light the chandeliers and snuff out the candles on the tree."

Millie nodded, pleased with this plan. "Then we shall pass out the presents for the children and . . ."

"What is it, Millie?" Vanessa gave the girl an anxious glance as her voice trailed off in mid sentence.

"I am just considering the disposal of the candles on the tree." Millie wore a most thoughtful expression. "Do the families in the village have need of candles, Prudence?"

Prudence nodded. "Indeed, they do. Most make tallow candles themselves, and they are used sparingly."

"And these will be wax, will they not?" Millie looked to her brother for the answer. When he nodded, a delighted smile spread across her face. "Let us make a ceremony of presenting each family with a wax candle from the tree."

"What a lovely idea!" Vanessa smiled at her excited friend, impressed with Millie's thoughtfulness. Then she turned to Stephen with a question. "Are there enough candles so every family can receive one?"

Stephen exchanged a speaking look with Vanessa. "If there are not, there will be. I will see to that. When will the children receive their presents?"

"Right after that, I should think." Prudence smiled. "We would not want the younger children to become too sleepy to admire their treasures. You will distribute the gifts, will you not, Millie?"

Millie raised her brows. "Me? I thought *you* would present the gifts."

"I will assist you with the names, of course, but you should be the one to present them. It would mean so much to the children."

Vanessa watched Millie carefully, recognizing only too well the shy and embarrassed expression that swept over her face. But Millie surprised her pleasantly.

"Of course I shall do it, if you think it best. I should like to see young Billie Draper's face when he sees the huge elephant I have made for him. Let us wrap each present in colored paper and write the child's name on the package. Then I will know how to address them, for I should like to say something of a personal nature to each child."

Prudence nodded and turned to Mr. Holland. "Will you assist us, Mr. Holland? Only an hour remains before teatime, and I should like us to be finished by then. My father is coming to tea, and I am eager for Millie to meet him."

"Of course I'll assist you." Mr. Holland smiled at them. "You say your father is coming here, Prudence?"

"Yes, he promised. He wished to make Millie's acquaintance, since I have spent the best part of the past five weeks here at Bridgeford Hall."

Millie smiled at Prudence as they linked arms with Mr. Holland and walked quickly toward the door. "I have wanted to make his acquaintance since you told me he once grew an orange tree from a seed. The head gardener said it was nearly impossible, and I wish to ask him how he achieved it."

Their voices trailed off as they exited the ballroom and went down the staircase together. When Vanessa turned to Stephen, she found him smiling at her.

"Where is my shy, retiring young sister?" Stephen took her arm and walked with her to the door. "It seems Millie has become quite a gadabout."

Vanessa nodded, smiling proudly. "She seemed a bit shy when Prudence first suggested she give out the presents, but she agreed quite readily to do so. And I noticed she did not seem at all disconcerted when she learned the rector was coming to tea."

"But you are not certain she is ready to enjoy a Season in London?"

Vanessa enjoyed the teasing grin that hovered about the corners of his lips. "I will admit I am *becoming* more certain."

"Why do you hesitate?" Stephen covered her hand with his own and gave it a gentle squeeze. "Even if Millie becomes quite self-sufficient, I should like you to stay here as long as you desire. Millie and I consider you a member of our family."

Vanessa's eyes widened with shock. "I would not hold Millie back because I fear for my own future!"

"I never doubted that." Stephen recaptured her hand, holding it firmly. "Millie appears quite normal to me."

"And to me. But we have not seen her in a true social situation as yet. She rubs along well with Prudence, but Prudence is much friendlier than the young ladies Millie might meet in London. And then there are the young gentlemen to consider. Millie has never made the acquaintance of any gentleman her age."

"Yes, it is true," Stephen agreed. "But you cannot fault me for hoping her shyness has passed."

"No, indeed. And I share your hope." Vanessa smiled as she looked up into his concerned eyes. "But we must reserve our opinion until she meets other young ladies and young gentlemen at the Christmas celebration. Only then will we know whether we should push Millie from the nest."

Stephen chuckled. "No doubt that is another of your colorful country references."

"It is." Vanessa's eyes sparkled. "It is the action mother birds take when it is time for their babies to fly. I have always regarded it as a bit drastic, and I would rather test Millie's wings at the Christmas celebration before we shove her out."

Six

The night of the Christmas celebration, Vanessa watched proudly as Millie accepted the arm of the squire's son. Stephen's sister had a new gown for the occasion, a lovely white silk with a white tissue overskirt shot through with gold threads. She wore gold silk ribbons in her glossy brown hair. To Vanessa, she looked like a Christmas angel as she awaited the beginning of the country dance.

Millie's shyness had not disappeared, but it was no longer crippling. She had distributed the presents with impressive grace, taking time to talk to each child. Only Vanessa had noticed her color was a bit higher than usual and her fingers trembled slightly as she passed the colorful packages into eager hands.

Her smile had been a bit strained at first, but the squeals of the delighted children made her eyes sparkle and her lips turn up in genuine happiness. When Prudence called for a round of applause for Lady Thurston and her brother, the ninth Earl of Bridgeford, Millie had positively beamed at the entire assembly.

The Christmas feast had presented no problem, even though Millie had been seated between the squire's eldest sons, both unmarried and her contemporaries in age. Millie exchanged polite pleasantries with the young gentlemen. When they discovered a mutual interest in designing a greenhouse that could withstand the harsh English winters and produce fruits year round, the final trace of her reticence vanished.

On the whole, Vanessa thought, the Christmas celebration was a huge success. The children had been delighted to find a score of entertainments arranged solely for them and had gone off to see the puppeteers and watch the magician quite eagerly. The youngest children were now asleep on their cots under the careful supervision of the nannies, and the parents were taking part in the dancing with a pleasure that was quite apparent.

Indeed, there had been only one unplanned incident, and Vanessa blushed to think of it. It occurred when Millie had passed out the last of the presents. At the bottom of her basket, she'd found an envelope.

"This is for you, Vanessa!" Millie had called out gaily, handing her the gold-colored envelope.

Vanessa had accepted it, recognizing the hand immediately. It was a missive from her secret admirer. Several guests, including her father, eyed her with curiosity, and she had given what she hoped was a casual smile. "No doubt it is a Christmas greeting from Lackington's Bookshop in London. I do believe I am their very best customer."

"Indeed, I believe you are." Mr. Holland had nodded, drawing the attention away from Vanessa. "If anyone should like to borrow Mrs. Burney's *Cecilia*, both Lady Thurston and my daughter have already read it, and it sits on the shelf at my cottage."

This had prompted a lively discussion on the advisability of perusing fiction, and Vanessa had exchanged a grateful glance with her father. The gold envelope had not been mentioned since, and it resided in the small reticule dangling from a loop round Vanessa's wrist.

"I say, you look quite fetching, Vanessa. At first glance, I could not believe it was you."

Vanessa turned to grin at George, who had retained his

habit of speaking first and thinking later, though Winnie had done her best to break him of the fault.

"Hello, George. Why are you not dancing with your wife?"

"She slipped down to the nursery to have a peek at the baby." George smiled proudly, precisely as the father of a new baby girl should. "Did you see her? She is every bit as pretty as Winnie."

Vanessa nodded. "I did, and you are quite right, George. Little Angela is the prettiest baby I have ever seen, and Winnie is a most contented mother and wife."

"How about you?" George's eyes crinkled with good humor and the effects of more than one glass of the champagne punch. "Have you found a good bloke to court you yet?"

Vanessa laughed. George's words had a sting, but it was not intentional. "Not yet, but not for lack of trying. Perhaps next year."

"Perhaps tonight. You look uncommonly pretty, not at all like your old self. The green of gown brings out the color of your eyes."

"It is new." Vanessa glanced down at her gown, a lovely draping of dark green velvet with a bodice cut so low she had filled it in with a bit of cream-colored Belgian lace. "It was a Christmas gift from the earl."

George gave a low whistle, his eyes roaming over the fine velvet fabric. "A handsome fellow and generous, too, to give this party for the whole village. And it's right handy for you, being as you're living here and all. Is that the direction the wind blows?"

"No, George." Vanessa hoped her cheeks were not reddening in embarrassment. "We are merely friends, just as you and I are. And do not forget, the earl has a wife."

"A wife we've never set eyes on. S'likely she thinks she's too good for the likes of us."

"She is ill." Vanessa kept her voice deliberately low. She

did not think George would cause a scene, but it was best to appear to be pleasant.

"All the same, he must be lonely, living here by himself and her off wherever she is. I know I'm sticking my foot in, Vanessa, but you could do a lot worse. No doubt he'd set you up for life if you offered him the companionship he desires."

Vanessa clamped her lips shut and counted to ten before she answered. "No. The earl is an honorable gentleman. He would never ask me to do anything improper. It is foolish for you to even think along those lines."

"Perhaps." George shrugged, then grinned as he caught sight of his wife at the ballroom door. "There's Winnie now. I promised to dance with her when she came back."

"Give her my greetings, George. I will attempt to find her later so she can tell me the latest news."

Instead of turning and making his way to his wife, George hesitated and looked quite ill at ease. "Don't tell her what I said, will you, Vanessa? She'd be in a high dudgeon if she knew I'd talked to you so personal like. We just want to see you happy and settled and all. We get together every month or so and try to come up with a husband for you. I guess it's because we're so happy, and . . . well . . . you do understand, don't you?"

"Indeed, I do." Vanessa watched him weave his way across the floor to join Winnie. She knew her friends hoped she would marry, but she had not known they met regularly to discuss it.

After a final glance at Millie, who was dancing with Winnie's younger brother, Vanessa wove her way through the merry crowd to the French doors that led out to the balcony. After stopping to converse with several guests on her way, including Prudence's mama and the rector, Vanessa at last achieved her goal. She stepped out into the chill night air and gave a grateful sigh as she hurried down the steps to the garden below. There had been no time to fetch a wrap, but Vanessa welcomed the embrace of the crisp frosty air. The heat of the ballroom had been oppressive, though the windows had been opened wide to the night.

Soon she arrived at the fountain. Small lanterns with colored glass panels illuminated the area to keep any guests from stumbling blindly into the puddle the fountain created.

Seating herself on a marble bench, Vanessa retrieved the envelope from her reticule. Holding it close to one of the lanterns, she extracted the letter, which was written on lovely, gold-colored paper, and read the words her unknown suitor had written.

My darling Vanessa, the letter began, causing Vanessa's cheeks to burn. A gentleman did not call an unmarried miss by her given name unless he was either a close relative or the young lady's fiancé.

> *I wish you the happiest Christmas, my dearest. I had thought to send you a small present as a token of my affections, but I did not wish to embarrass you in front of your friends. Instead, I will tell you the secret of the gold heart you wear around your lovely throat. You no doubt think the gold prongs in the center are merely a rosebud, but their appearance is deceiving. They are fashioned to hold a gem to match your sparkling green eyes.*

Vanessa frowned slightly. Was this so? She had assumed the beautiful gold pendant was complete just as it was. She turned back to the letter again, and her eyes widened as she read the next lines.

> *I have found the perfect gem, dear Vanessa, and I shall present it to you on Valentine's Day. You will note I promised to present it, not send it to you. I must make my pres-*

ence known to you, as I cannot wait any longer. If the time is right on Valentine's Day, I shall ask for your hand in marriage, for I love you above all others. You are the only lady I wish to call my wife.

"Oh, my!" Vanessa's hands flew up to her cheeks, which were hot despite the chill air. She read the letter again, her face flaming in the light of the lantern, and then drew out the gold heart pendant to see if her secret admirer's words were true.

With trembling fingers, Vanessa unclasped the chain and held the gold heart up to the light. The furled petals of the rosebud were indeed fashioned to hold a gem.

"Vanessa." The deep voice behind her caused Vanessa to whirl around in surprise. "Why did you leave the celebration?"

Vanessa hurriedly composed herself and managed to smile at Stephen. "I simply wished for a bit of . . . of air."

"And what is this?" Stephen took the pendant from her trembling fingers and held it up to the light. "Lovely. Is it from an admirer?"

Vanessa nodded, the color rising to her cheeks again. She was well and truly caught out, and she would not lie to Stephen. "Yes, it is."

"The squire's son, perhaps?" Stephen grinned at her and Vanessa realized he was watching her closely.

"No. It is from . . ." Vanessa stopped, uncertain how to continue. She had experienced several pangs of guilt when she fabricated the Banbury tale for her father, and she had vowed never to indulge in the same sort of deceit again.

"You do not wish to tell me?" Stephen smiled and took her hand. "Perhaps I am wrong to ask you to reveal your secret."

Vanessa took a deep breath as she shook her head. "No.

I would tell you if I could, but my admirer *is* secret. He has chosen to hide his identity from me."

"A secret admirer," Stephen said. "But you harbor some suspicion?"

"No, I do not. At first I thought it was a prank."

Stephen frowned. "A prank? But why?"

"I am not the type of pretty, fluff-headed miss who inspires such devotion in a gentleman. Just look at me, Stephen. I am twenty-six years old and firmly on the shelf. No one has ever declared for me, or expressed the slightest interest in doing so."

"But there must have been . . ."

"No." Vanessa interrupted before he could continue. "It is understandable, and I do not mind. Not only do I have more height than any gentleman in Bridgeford Village, but I also engage in unladylike pursuits."

Stephen raised his brows. "You do?"

"Yes, indeed. I study subjects better left to gentlemen, go walking alone through the woods, and seldom suffer fools with a smile. It is not surprising no man would choose me for his wife."

"You are quite mistaken, Vanessa. Some man *does* want you for his wife. You simply do not know who he is."

"I do not believe it." Vanessa chuckled. "Who would want a wife like me? I know my failings well, sir, and I am not even pretty."

"That is true. You are not pretty in the traditional sense. Your face has far too much character to be merely pretty. But you *are* beautiful. You need but glance in the mirror. Your reflection will prove me correct."

Stephen's comment left Vanessa mute. Was he attempting to flatter her into a more pleasant frame of mind, or did he truly find her beautiful?

"You have the face and form of a marble, Vanessa, an ancient goddess of grace, beauty, and strength."

Though she was pleased he should think so, Vanessa

could not help but smile at his description. "You are kindness itself, and your compliment is lovely. But no mortal man would choose to marry a goddess. Why, she might become angry with him and turn him into a toad."

"She might." Stephen chuckled. "But he should deserve his fate for displeasing her. Did your unknown admirer tell you the purpose of the rosebud in the center of this heart?"

Vanessa nodded, relieved Stephen had turned their discussion to another subject. "Yes, the petals are prongs designed to hold a gem. He writes he will present it to me when he asks for my hand in marriage."

"And will you accept him?"

There was a curious note in Stephen's voice that Vanessa could not ignore. "Most certainly not! Though I am of the age to be considered a spinster, I am not so unhappy with my unmarried state that I should purchase a horse without first checking its teeth."

Stephen chuckled, and the sound of his mirth in the deserted garden made Vanessa smile.

"The teeth of a horse tell much about its age and health, sir, but is not precisely what I meant. I must meet this gentleman before I decide whether or not to pursue our acquaintance."

Stephen nodded. "That does seem wise. But you *did* accept his gift. Are you receptive to his advances?"

"Not at all." Vanessa laughed. "I did not know where to return it. And since it is charming, I have decided to wear it until he presents himself. If he is equally charming, I may decide to keep it."

"And if he is not as charming as his gift?"

"I shall return it with the greatest haste."

"I see," Stephen said. "I cannot fault you on your reasoning, Vanessa. Now, if you would turn slightly and lift your hair, I shall clasp your lovely gift around your neck."

"Thank you." Vanessa lifted her hair and turned so her back was to him. As his warm fingers brushed the back of her neck, a delicious tingle of excitement swept through her, and she was grateful he could not see her face.

"There. It is done." Stephen took her arm and turned her so they again faced one another. "Now there is another question I must ask you. How did you find Millie's comportment this evening?"

Vanessa smiled, grateful they had gone on to matters less personal. "I found her behavior quite admirable. She is still a bit shy around strangers, of course, but it lends her a charming and gentle air."

"Then she need not wait another year to have her Season in London?"

Vanessa considered the query. "No. I believe she is as ready as she will ever be. Millie's first Season shall either kill or cure her."

"Good heavens!" Stephen gave a startled laugh. "Surely it is not so serious as all that. What could be so difficult about a few balls and parties?"

Vanessa frowned. "It will be difficult indeed if she has no friends. Millie will feel like nothing so much as a trout in sand."

"A trout in sand?" Stephen laughed again. "Explain yourself, Vanessa."

"I simply meant she would be out of her element. Nothing is more frightening to a shy young miss than entering a room filled with strangers. If you do send Millie to London for the Season, I would caution you to make certain she makes the acquaintance of several friendly young misses well in advance of her first party."

"Yes." Stephen nodded. "That would be wise. Do you have any other cautions?"

Vanessa smiled. "You must guard Millie carefully, for

she might not recognize a civet in the guise of a tame parlor cat."

Stephen threw back his head and gave a hearty laugh. "Again, I desire an explanation."

"As an innocent, Millie may be so impressed with the trappings of town bronze she may fail to use good judgment in selecting her suitors. I merely meant someone must assist her in identifying the fortune hunters and the empty-headed dandies."

Stephen hugged her tightly. "You have made valid points, Vanessa. I shall keep them in mind when I make the arrangements for Millie's London debut."

Vanessa sighed, enjoying the safe embrace of his strong arms for a moment. She pulled back, a smile on her face. "You must not be anxious, Stephen. I have great confidence in Millie's abilities. With the proper guidance, she shall sail through her London Season with all the elegance you could possibly desire."

Seven

On the day before the new year, Vanessa was enjoying the large, comfortable chamber that housed Bridgeford Hall's library. She had just shelved several recent acquisitions when she heard footsteps racing down the passageway toward the library door. She turned, curious about the reason for such haste. Millie burst into the chamber.

"Millie! Your face is quite flushed." Vanessa thought at first that Millie was ill. Her color was high and her breathing much quicker than normal, but her eyes were not lackluster, as in one who suffered from a fever. Instead, they were sparkling and a smile turned up the corners of her lips.

"I am so happy I can scarcely speak. Stephen has just told me we are to go to London for the Season!"

"That is wonderful news." Vanessa returned her excited smile, hoping Millie would not be too distressed when she learned Vanessa was not to accompany her. "When will you leave?"

"In less than a week. Stephen has promised to take us to all sorts of marvelous places. We shall go to Astley's Circus and Vauxhall Gardens, and we shall even have a box at the theatre! And of course we shall spend hours in Lackington's Bookshop. You are eager to see it, are you not, Vanessa?"

"Yes, I am. But . . ."

"Stephen has asked me to send you to him," Millie

interrupted. "No doubt he wishes to make further arrangements with you. You had best hurry. Several gentlemen are waiting to see him, and he is quite pressed for time."

Vanessa nodded. It was not wise to tell Millie she was to go to London alone and then leave her to deal with the disappointment by herself. After her conference with Stephen, there would be time to comfort Millie and assure her all young ladies of quality must leave their country companions behind when they went off to London for the Season.

"I shall go up and examine my wardrobe while you are closeted with Stephen." With a final smile, Millie turned and headed for the door. "He advised me to take only my newest gowns, as he has already engaged the very best French modiste in London to outfit us for the Season."

Vanessa sighed as Millie rushed out of the library and ran off in the direction of the grand staircase. The girl believed Vanessa would accompany her. It would be Vanessa's unpleasant duty to disabuse her of that notion.

Taking a deep, steadying breath, Vanessa left the library and walked down the passageway to Stephen's study. Since the door was ajar, she slipped in quietly and stood in front of his desk, waiting for him to acknowledge her presence.

"Vanessa." Stephen looked up from his pile of correspondence and rose to his feet, smiling. "Let us move to our favorite chairs, and I will tell you what arrangements I have made for Millie's Season."

Vanessa sat in the chair he indicated and accepted the small glass of sherry he poured for her. She sipped a small bit out of politeness, but set the glass down at the first opportunity, knowing she would need a clear head to deal with Millie's disappointment.

"Millie appeared quite delighted when I told her she was to have a Season in London." Stephen looked relieved. "I had thought she might be anxious, but she seemed most pleased with the opportunity to see new sights."

Vanessa nodded. "You are right. She was bubbling with enthusiasm over the entertainments she would enjoy. But I fear Millie is unaware I will not be traveling to London. I think it best if I tell her promptly so she will become accustomed to the idea."

"There is no need for that." Stephen's eyes twinkled. "You see, Vanessa, I have arranged for your first Season to take place at the very same time. You and Millie will be presented together."

For a moment, Vanessa was too shocked to speak. She stared at him in confusion. "Have you forgotten my station?"

"Your station is about to change, and the daughter of a baron is certainly entitled to have a Season."

"A *baron?*"

Stephen grinned, reaching for her hand and patting it lightly. "Your father is to be recognized by the Crown for his scholarly works. It is a title only and conveys no accompanying lands, but it is no small honor. It is highly unusual for the Crown to create a new barony."

"Papa is to be a baron?" Vanessa was so shocked she was nearly rendered speechless. "But . . . why? How?"

"King George was most impressed when he learned your father's writings were widely read at both Cambridge and Oxford, and he felt some honor should be accorded. And when Queen Charlotte found you had rendered the illustrations for your father's books, she requested you be presented to her."

"I am to be presented to the Queen?" Vanessa felt her lips part and shape a perfectly round circle of surprise. "But . . . are you certain?"

"Yes. Queen Charlotte charged me with the happy duty of transporting you to London and delivering you to her Presentation Chamber in two weeks' time."

Vanessa drew a deep breath and expelled it in awe. "Perhaps I should pinch myself to make certain I am not dreaming. Never, not in my wildest dreams, did I imagine I should be presented to my Queen."

"There is more." Stephen clearly enjoyed her amazement. "Her Majesty wishes you to view a new rose that has been named in her honor. Her gardeners tell her it should be in full bloom in two weeks, and she instructed me to tell you she would consider it a great favor if you would render a sketch of it for her."

Vanessa shook her head to clear it. Then she gazed at him quite sharply. "You must be bamming me, Stephen! Do you truly expect me to believe Queen Charlotte wishes to have one of my sketches?"

"I do. And after you have been duly presented and rendered your sketch, you shall stay in London to enjoy the Season with Millie—not as her companion, but as a fellow debutante. Your father has already given his permission, so you need have no worries on score."

Vanessa's mind spun, and she gripped the arms of the chair tightly. "I fear a Season for me would be quite impossible, Stephen. I have the means for a presentation gown, as I have put aside most of my wages, but I shall not ask Papa to deplete his purse on my account. I must return to Bridgeford Village immediately after the ceremony so as not to incur additional expenses."

"I shall stand the cost of your Season, Vanessa. Your father and I have already agreed."

"*You?*" Vanessa stared up at him in shock. "But that would not be proper! What would people think if . . ."

"They will think nothing of it. You are in my employ, and it is only right I stand the cost of your Season."

"But I am *not* in your employ. You said yourself I would go to London as a debutante, not as Millie's companion."

"That is neither here nor there." Stephen grinned at

her. "Or, as you often say, neither fish nor fowl. You see, I have need of your services on Millie's behalf."

Vanessa's frown deepened. "I cannot imagine how I could possibly be of assistance. I know nothing of fashion or society, and Millie has no need of my nursing skills."

Stephen laughed. "You are overlooking the most important service of all. You can be Millie's friend. You cautioned me to find a friend for Millie so she will not feel like a trout in sand, did you not?"

"Yes, but one cannot buy friendship. One may hire a maid and a footman and pay them wages, but one does not hire a friend."

"That is true, but there is a second service you must perform for Millie. You expressed doubts she would recognize civets dressed up as tame parlor cats. I should like you to be on the lookout for any such creatures and protect Millie from them."

Vanessa stared at him for a moment and then burst into laughter. "You wish to engage my services as a civet detector?"

"I do." Stephen nodded gravely.

Vanessa noticed the twinkle in his eye and could not resist the urge to tease him a bit. "I have never attempted such a position before. How will you know if I am accurate in my detection?"

"You will be. I cannot imagine any civet could be clever enough to trick you."

Vanessa shrugged. "Perhaps not. Papa has always claimed I have an uncanny knack for discerning a person's true nature."

"Then you will agree to stay in London and guard Millie against these society civets?"

Vanessa nodded. "Of course, if you judge I am needed."

"It is settled, then. I cannot be with Millie constantly,

and though my mama-in-law will do her best, it would relieve my mind to know you are also by her side."

"Your mama-in-law?" Vanessa raised her brows in surprise. Stephen had never mentioned his wife's family before.

Stephen nodded. "Lady Treverton is an undisputed leader of the *ton*, and she shall instruct you and Millie how to go on in society. Though she is quite modest and may not mention it, I know she was deemed an Incomparable during her own first Season."

"Oh, my!" Vanessa was impressed. "I do hope Millie and I will not disappoint her."

"I am certain you will not. Lady Treverton has absented herself from society for the past several years, but when I told her about you and Millie, she immediately offered to bring both of you out. She insisted you stay with her for the Season."

"That is exceedingly kind of her." Vanessa did her best to hide her curiosity. "Lady Treverton is a widow, then?"

A flicker of pain crossed Stephen's face, and she wished she had not asked the question. But he composed himself instantly.

"No, Vanessa. Lord Treverton is very much alive. But he suffered an accident that has left him bedridden and quite debilitated. It occurred several years ago. Since that time, Lady Treverton has devoted all her waking moments to his care. Only recently has she found a nurse to relieve her of some of the duties."

"It must have been very difficult for her." Vanessa felt an instant sympathy for Lady Treverton. She was well acquainted with the strain of nursing an invalid and the depression that often resulted from witnessing a loved one's failing health. "Are you certain the task of supervising two very green debutantes will not overtax her strength?"

"I should think your presence would have quite the

opposite effect. I expect you and Millie will provide some much-needed diversion for Lady Treverton and a good reason to take her out of the sickroom and into society again. You see, Vanessa, before his unfortunate accident, Lord and Lady Treverton were among the most popular members of the *ton*. Invitations to their parties were highly coveted, and I am convinced Lady Treverton misses the companionship of her society friends."

"Then we shall stay with her, of course. Perhaps I could even help her in caring for Lord Treverton."

Stephen shook his head. "No. Lord Treverton has withdrawn from society completely. He refuses to see any of his former friends. The only persons admitted to his chambers are his wife, his nurse, and me."

"I see." Vanessa said, though she did not see at all. What manner of accident had Lord Treverton suffered to turn him into such a recluse?

"Lady Treverton has been morose of late, and I am certain she will benefit from having two lively debutantes under her roof. I have not forgotten what a miracle you wrought with Millie, and I wish you to do the same for Lady Treverton. I am hopeful your presence will provide her with some welcome levity."

Vanessa nodded. Stephen was fond of his mama-in-law and concerned for her welfare. "That should not be difficult. I expect Lady Treverton shall burst into gales of laughter the moment she sets eyes on me."

"But why?" Stephen looked puzzled. "You are a well-mannered and highly accomplished young lady."

"Perhaps, but I should like you to imagine the current crowd of debutantes. Will they not be pretty and dainty and dressed in clouds of lacy white for their come-out balls?"

"Yes." He nodded. "It is always done in that fashion."

Vanessa's grin widened. "I have no doubt Millie shall fit in nicely. I am another matter."

"I do not understand your point. If you are concerned about your appearance, you may put fear to rest. I will see to it you are dressed in the first stare of fashion."

"I never doubted that for a moment." Vanessa chuckled softly and rose to her feet so her stature was more clearly visible. "Now I wish you to picture me, in your mind's eye, dressed similarly and in the very center of this charming group of dainty young hopefuls. Do you not find something quite ridiculous about this vision?"

Stephen's lips twitched up and Vanessa knew he had taken her point. "But, Vanessa, you are lovely. I have often remarked on it most sincerely. Perhaps your beauty is not in the current fashion, but . . ."

"Thank you, Stephen." Vanessa interrupted his hasty reassurances and smiled down at him kindly. "I know what I am, and I am not in the least self-conscious as to my form or my height. But I should think Lady Treverton might find it easier to hide a horse in a field of cows than make a charming young debutante of me."

Eight

"You were wonderful, Vanessa." Millie cast her an admiring glance as they lifted their lacy white skirts and hoops and hastened up the grand staircase in Lord and Lady Treverton's mansion. "We were the envy of everyone there when Queen Charlotte singled us out for her attentions."

Vanessa nodded. "The other debutantes did appear envious. Lady Christina Evanston, in particular, seemed in quite a pout."

"She is the daughter of a marquis." Millie reached the top step and led the way down the passageway. "No doubt she thought she should be afforded more of Her Majesty's attention than the daughters of an earl and a lesser baron. Her complexion turned a most unbecoming shade when Queen Charlotte instructed the palace footman to take us to her private rose conservatory and stated her intent to join us there the moment she had discharged her duties."

Vanessa could not help the impish smile that played merrily with the corners of her lips. When they had arrived at St. James's Palace, they had been shown to the long hall to await the Queen's summons. Lady Christina had been in the group of other debutantes scheduled to be presented, and she had been pointedly rude when she learned she outranked Millie and Vanessa. "I agree Lady

Christina received precisely what she deserved, but it is not kind of us to gloat."

"You are right. Gloating should not become us. But it *was* gratifying, was it not?"

"Extremely." Vanessa grinned, halting at the door to Millie's bedchamber. "Let us change out of our presentation gowns, Millie. When we are more comfortably dressed, I shall join you in our sitting room and we shall ring for tea."

Millie nodded. "Perhaps we should request a light nuncheon. Are you also sharp set?"

"Indeed, I am. I was so anxious at breakfast I could eat very little."

"You were anxious?" Millie turned to gaze at her in astonishment. "I should never have guessed it. You appeared to me to be entirely composed."

Vanessa laughed. "Appearances are deceiving. I did not mention it, for fear you would also become anxious, but my heart was fluttering as rapidly as a hummingbird's wings."

"But you were not anxious when we met Queen Charlotte in her garden. At least, I do not think you were. Your fingers were not trembling when you rendered your sketch."

"I was not anxious then. I had already been presented, you see, and I had not tripped on my train, made a muddle of my curtsy, or experienced any other of the disasters I imagined might occur. I do believe anticipation is much more nerve-racking than the actual performance of the deed."

Millie stopped with her hand on the door and looked very thoughtful. "You are quite right, Vanessa. Once one is thrust into the middle of a situation, there is nothing for it but to carry on. I shall remember that when we make our entrance this evening, for I must admit I am anxious."

"What is the worst that can happen?" Vanessa smiled at her.

Millie sighed. "I could embarrass myself in the receiving line by forgetting a notable's name."

"Impossible. The guests will be announced. All you need do is listen to the names."

"I had forgotten that. But there is the dancing to consider. What if no gentleman asks me to dance?"

"That is also impossible. Stephen will partner you in the first dance and he will hand you over to the next young gentleman who has signed your dance card. You will not lack for partners, Millie. Every young gentleman in attendance will come forward to dance with Lady Treverton's protégée."

"You have come close to relieving my fears."

"Close?" Vanessa smiled at Millie's turn of phrase. "What other fears do you entertain?"

"The dancing itself. What if I tread on my partner's toes?"

"Your partner will apologize, of course, for dancing so clumsily. He will accept the fault as his own, even if it is yours."

"Perhaps there are some advantages to being a debutante after all." Millie smiled. "Still, I find I am anticipating the conclusion of the evening with much more pleasure than the beginning."

"It will not be as bad as *that*. But if you have reason to desire a respite from the ballroom, I have learned a trick from one of the maids."

"You have? You must tell me."

Vanessa grinned at her. "All you need do is rip loose a few stitches on your skirt."

A puzzled expression fled over Millie's face. "But . . . why would I rip my skirt?"

"So it must be mended, of course. You will simply excuse yourself and send one of the footmen to fetch me.

Then the two of us shall repair to the ladies' withdrawing room to enjoy a comfy coze while one of the maids plies her needle."

"That is deliciously devious." Millie laughed in delight. "You may be certain I shall remember a ploy so useful as that. No doubt I shall rely on it often."

"But make use of this subterfuge only once of an evening. Any more and you will ruin the reputation of our modiste."

"I shall remember, Vanessa." Millie smiled and hurried into her bedchamber, calling out for her abigail to attend her. Vanessa continued down the passageway and entered her own chamber, lifting the feathered headdress from her hair and giving a sigh of relief. They had accomplished their presentations without mishap, and Her Majesty had been quite kind, praising Vanessa's sketch most highly. She had also expressed her approval when Vanessa said the colored drawing would be completed within the week and delivered to St. James's Palace.

Rather than wait for assistance, Vanessa struggled out of her traditional gown and hoops. She hung the elaborate and regrettably old-fashioned gown in her clothespress and made a mental note to send it to Mrs. Draggit, the blacksmith's wife, who could use the fabric to make several fine gowns for her growing daughters. Then she sank down in the comfortable chair by her window, tucking her feet up and giving way to the exhaustion that had assailed her for the past several days.

They had departed for London on the third day following Vanessa's conversation with Stephen. It had been a journey of four hours and they'd arrived at Lord and Lady Treverton's mansion by teatime none the worse for wear. This was due in no small part to the new family coach Stephen had purchased, a well-sprung conveyance, luxuriously equipped.

Vanessa had found herself trembling slightly as they en-

tered the opulent mansion in Callendar Square. She had
assumed Lady Treverton would welcome them at the door,
but the stiffly proper butler, Mr. Hodges, showed them
directly to their chambers so they might wash off the dust
of the road and make themselves presentable before they
met his mistress.

She had been pleased to discover she and Millie were
to share a suite of rooms. They had separate bedchambers
and dressing rooms at either end of the suite, but between
them was a large and well-appointed sitting room they
were to share for the length of their stay. This was where
Lady Treverton would join them.

Once Vanessa and Millie had tidied themselves, they
met in the sitting room. Several moments later, the door
opened and a lovely older woman, wearing the most beautiful gown Vanessa had ever seen, entered the chamber
and announced she was their hostess.

Vanessa and Millie had curtsied, unsure of how to address her, but Lady Treverton quickly set them at their
ease. To call her Lady Treverton should be much too formal, she said, and Lady Eulalia put her in mind of the
strange yodels Swiss shepherds used in the Alps. As Lady
Lolly was far too silly for words, she had decided Aunt
Lolly would be just the thing.

Aunt Lolly was not the least bit formidable, and both
Vanessa and Millie had grown to like her very well indeed.
She had taken them in hand, declaring herself delighted
with the prospect of bringing them out, but warning them
she had arranged only one Season before, that of her
stepdaughter.

Vanessa's brows had lifted in surprise. Stephen's wife
was not her daughter? Aunt Lolly had smiled. When she'd
married the widowed Lord Treverton, his daughter,
Phoebe, had already been fifteen years of age. Her stepdaughter's first Season had been very successful. Aunt

Lolly promised them she would spare no effort to achieve the same success for them.

The next several days had flown by quickly, filled from dawn to dusk with activities. Aunt Lolly had engaged a tutor to teach them court protocol and etiquette, a daunting subject indeed. There was also a dancing master to give them lessons in the steps they would need to perform and a music instructor to improve their skills upon the lovely pianoforte in the Treverton's music room. Once Millie and Vanessa had been properly outfitted and polished, Aunt Lolly declared they were ready, and they had gone off to St. James's Palace to be presented to their Queen.

This first, very necessary step had been accomplished, and Vanessa was relieved. Her Majesty had recognized them in the solemn ceremony, and now they were truly debutantes. This evening, they would be Aunt Lolly's guests of honor at their come-out ball, and once the ball had concluded, their Seasons would commence.

Vanessa sighed, already dreading the round of parties and balls she would be required to attend. They were to be given a slight respite, as the true Season did not begin until the opening of parliament some seven weeks hence.

During this lull, Aunt Lolly had planned for them to attend the opera, Astley's Circus, Vauxhall Gardens, and Almack's. They would shop for the necessities they had not yet purchased, go riding in Hyde Park, and peruse the volumes at Lackington's Bookshop. They would also attend smaller gatherings given by families who had remained in London and not repaired to their country estates.

Once the true Season began, there would be little time for ordinary amusements, as they would be deluged with invitations. Aunt Lolly told them during her own first Season she attended fifty balls, sixty parties, thirty dinners, and twenty-five Venetian breakfasts. The thought of all those engagements made Vanessa's head whirl. She sighed as she slipped into the lovely dark green silk wrapper Aunt Lolly had commissioned for her, pulled on soft slippers of the same hue, tied her hair back with a dark green ribbon, and opened the sitting room door to find Millie and Aunt Lolly waiting for her.

"Vanessa, dear." Aunt Lolly rose to embrace her. "Millie has just told me how well you were received by Her Majesty. I expected both of you to do well, of course, but I had no notion Queen Charlotte would spirit you off for a private audience."

Vanessa smiled, the color rising to her cheeks at the compliment. "She did seem quite enamored of my sketch, Aunt Lolly. And I do not think she took offense when I asked if she suffered the headache."

"Is *that* what you were discussing when she drew you aside to look at the rest of her garden?" Millie's eyes widened. "You did not tell me."

"It was of little consequence. I merely remarked she appeared to be in pain and asked her if she could describe its nature. When she did, I suggested a simple remedy."

"You suggested a remedy to Her Majesty?" Aunt Lolly's brows rose with surprise.

"Of course. No one need suffer from the headache when there is a cure. Her Majesty seemed quite impressed when I told her precisely how to prepare a tea of willow bark. She even wondered aloud why her court physician had not prescribed it."

"And what did you say to that?" Aunt Lolly winced slightly.

"You needn't worry, Aunt Lolly. I was perfectly polite. I told her he might not know of the remedy, as Papa and I had learned it from an old Gypsy healer. And then I said most physicians regard themselves as quite above simple country remedies. They tend to regard a dose of laudanum as the answer to every complaint."

"And did Her Majesty answer you?" Aunt Lolly's voice was shaking slightly.

"She laughed and told me laudanum was precisely what he had prescribed for her, but she did not care for the strong effects of the drug. I assured her willow bark tea would not make her the least bit sleepy or muddle-headed, and she thanked me for my advice."

Aunt Lolly's lips parted in amazement and she drew a deep breath. "Good heavens, Vanessa! Do you realize you usurped the authority of the court physician?"

"Perhaps." Vanessa was not in the least perturbed. "But I would not have been required to do so had he used a bit of common sense in the treatment he prescribed. Giving laudanum for the headache is like attempting to shell a walnut with a ten-pound mallet."

"I have no doubt is true, but a young miss who has just been presented to her Queen does not usually offer medical advice. It is amazing Her Majesty was not overset with you for . . ."

Aunt Lolly stopped speaking as one of her footmen entered, bearing a silver salver containing a letter. "This just arrived for Miss Holland, m'lady. One of the Queen's footmen delivered it."

"Are you certain, Harold?" When the footman nodded, Aunt Lolly's face turned pale and she turned to Vanessa, frowning. "You'd best open it, my dear."

Vanessa took the letter and broke the royal seal with trembling fingers. Had she breached etiquette by offering medical assistance to her Queen? She read it quickly and looked up with a relieved smile. "Her Majesty thanks me for my kind interest in her health and reports the willow bark tea was most helpful. She also states she is most pleased I broached the subject, as none other has had the courage to do so for fear of offending her."

"Good heavens, that's a relief! There will be no more etiquette lessons, Vanessa. From now on, you must behave exactly as you think best. You appear to rub along superbly on your own."

Vanessa raised her brows. "Are you certain, Aunt Lolly?"

"Indeed, I am." Aunt Lolly gave a decisive nod. "Other young misses have followed court protocol to the letter, and I daresay not one has received a personal letter of gratitude from her Queen."

Nine

"I am finished, Miss Vanessa." Colette, the French abigail Aunt Lolly had assigned to Millie and Vanessa, gave a final pat to Vanessa's coiffure. "You must open your eyes now and see if you approve of the way I have arranged your hair."

Vanessa nodded, sighing slightly. She had closed her eyes while Colette dressed her hair, not wishing to see the final result until the deed was accomplished. Aunt Lolly claimed Colette could perform magic with a brush and comb, but Vanessa doubted anyone, talented or not, could tame her unruly blond curls.

"Thank you, Colette." Vanessa opened her eyes and smiled at the diminutive lady's maid. "I have no doubt you did the very best you could, under the circumstances. My hair has always been most . . . oh, my!"

Colette laughed at Vanessa's astonished expression. "It is very elegant, no? One must let such delightful curls have their way. To attempt to confine them overmuch would be most foolish."

Vanessa nodded, staring at her reflection with awe. Somehow, Colette had managed to accomplish what she had long thought was impossible. Instead of drawing her hair back severely and brushing out the curls as Vanessa had always attempted to do, Colette had gathered the mass of curls loosely behind Vanessa's head and secured them with a clever gold circular clasp. The shining mass emerged from the center of the circlet to fall in ringlets to Vanessa's shoulders in a most becoming style.

"You have accomplished a miracle." Vanessa turned to the lady's maid in astonishment. "However did you manage this?"

Colette gave a very Gallic shrug, but her eyes sparkled merrily. "It is simply the clasp."

"I will own the clasp is part of the miracle." Vanessa turned her head to admire the clever design. "But you have placed it just so, and that makes you a miracle worker. I do wish I could meet the person who designed it. It is simply ingenious."

"Do you truly think so?"

"Indeed, I do." Vanessa noticed the look of pride on Colette's face and started to grin. "*You* designed it?"

Colette nodded, her lips turning up in a smile. "Lady Treverton asked me if I could design a clasp to hold your hair. When I finished my drawings, she took me to her jeweler and he fashioned it from gold."

"It is lovely." Vanessa turned her head to admire the clasp again. "Aunt Lolly must have been very pleased with you."

"She was. And the jeweler was most impressed. He said he would make several others to display in his window, and he promised Lady Treverton if they are purchased, he will share the profit with me."

"That's wonderful, Colette. Perhaps you will earn enough money to become a jewelry designer."

Colette shrugged. "Perhaps. My mama always told me whatever will be will be. Should you care to stand now so I may help you with your gown? Then we shall see the full effect."

"Of course." Vanessa rose to her feet, dwarfing the much smaller and daintier abigail. She grinned as the abigail fetched her gown and hopped up on the seat of a chair.

At Colette's nod, Vanessa stepped closer and the abigail slipped the gown over her head, taking great care not to dislodge any of her curls. Once this was accomplished, Colette fastened the gown and smoothed the lovely fabric in place.

"Ah! You are exquisite." Colette's lips turned up in a smile of approval as she climbed down from the chair. "Come look in the glass and you shall see there is no need for the rouge pot. Your cheeks bloom with roses on this night."

Vanessa stared with wonder at her reflection in the glass. It had not been difficult to convince Aunt Lolly she would look ridiculous in the lacy white gown that was almost *de rigueur* for a young lady's come-out ball. Indeed, that good lady had dissolved into gales of delighted laughter when Vanessa had declared that to dress her in white lace and present her as a demure young miss would be tantamount to dressing a foxhound in a tutu and declaring it to be a prima ballerina.

Now, dressed in the ball gown Aunt Lolly had commissioned for her, Vanessa could not help but admire her reflection. The sea-green silk matched the color of her eyes, and the extra height and flesh she had thought would set her apart from the rest of the guests was cleverly hidden by the cut and style of her dress. Indeed, she looked almost regal, precisely as Aunt Lolly had promised her. Though Vanessa knew full well she would not be the belle of the ball, her appearance would not embarrass either Millie or Aunt Lolly.

"Shall I clasp your lovely pendant around your neck?" Colette picked up the gold pendant and climbed up on the chair once again.

"Yes, thank you, Colette."

Vanessa drew on her gloves and took up a position in front of the chair. Colette settled the chain around her neck, clasped it securely, and then hopped down to hand her the lovely ivory fan Aunt Lolly had chosen. A moment later, wearing her matching slippers and clutching her reticule, Vanessa took a deep breath and left her chambers to join Millie and Aunt Lolly in the drawing room, where they would await their first guests.

As she lifted her skirts to descend the grand staircase, Vanessa found her heart was beating a rapid tattoo in her breast. She was not anxious over the ball. As long as she kept a tight curb on her tongue, took care to remember the proper manner in which to address the various lords and ladies, and recalled the progression of steps that made up the current dances, she should survive the evening without mishap.

Then why am I so overset? The moment the question popped into Vanessa's mind, she knew the answer. Stephen would be attending the ball, and the thought of him made her breath catch in her throat. She had not seen him since the day they arrived in London, and she missed him dreadfully. How would Stephen react to the sight of her in her finery? Would he tell her again she resembled a goddess? Or would he compare her with the younger, prettier debutantes and realize he had been mistaken?

Aunt Lolly had arranged for Stephen to lead Millie out for the first dance of the evening and favor Vanessa with the supper dance. Indeed, Vanessa did not know how she could keep a perfectly bland smile on her face and manage to utter the appropriate banalities, but somehow she must. She had to hide her emotions while the gentleman she loved held her in his arms under the careful scrutiny of his mother-in-law and the very proper notables of the *ton.*

Vanessa gave a relieved sigh as Millie danced with her fourth partner of the evening. Millie had been a bit anxious at first, but she had endured the lengthy reception line with a smile and more poise than Vanessa had known she possessed. The first dance had also gone well. While Millie danced with Stephen, Vanessa had taken the floor with Aunt Lolly's elderly uncle, a retired military gentleman who'd turned out to be a superb dancer. Unfortunately, he was quite short, but Vanessa had acquitted herself well even though the top of his head didn't rise past her chin.

Now, an hour into the festivities, Millie had not lacked a partner for a single dance, a fact that pleased Vanessa exceedingly well. She, on the other hand, had danced only once, but that did not signify. Vanessa had never expected an overly tall, unfashionable miss from the country to be the belle of the ball. That honor was reserved for Millie. It was enough for Vanessa to be included in Millie's magical evening.

She could not, however, stand motionless like a dolt. Vanessa brightened her smile and made her way through the crowded ballroom to a group of debutantes. She introduced herself quite properly, and they politely moved aside so she could join in their converse.

"Oh, look!" One of the debutantes, Miss Waxter, giggled shrilly. "That darling Mr. Woodhouse is dancing with Charity Plimpton!"

Another debutante, Honoria Collins, gazed in the direction Miss Waxter had pointed and frowned. "It is a complete *mésalliance*, if I do not say so myself. Whatever can he see in *her*?"

"Her papa's fortune!" A plump redhead, whose name Vanessa did not recall, gave a bray of laughter. "Do you not know Miss Plimpton's father used to be in trade?"

Miss Collins's eyes widened. "No! Are you certain, Henrietta?"

"Of course I am. He did not expect to inherit, you see, as he was only a cousin. He made his fortune in shipping, or some such common thing. I believe he received his title quite recently."

"Within the past year." Miss Waxter nodded sagely. "I heard Papa speak of it. He declared it unfortunate that the new baron could not change his background, for he appeared to be a decent enough fellow."

Miss Collins gave a dismissive wave of her fan. "Perhaps he should have thought of before he went into trade. Mama says it is far better for a gentleman to starve than to demean himself by taking up an unsuitable occupation."

Vanessa managed to keep the polite smile on her face, but she was sorely tempted to tell them what her own papa did for a living. She imagined their reaction to that startling piece of news, and her smile grew wider. To say someone should starve rather than take up honest work was absurd.

Miss Waxter gave another shrill giggle and Vanessa was tempted to cover her ears. "The gown she is wearing is a horror! Did no one to tell her red is not an appropriate color for a debutante?"

Vanessa glanced at Miss Plimpton again. To her eyes, the young lady's gown seemed lovely and contrasted nicely with her black hair and white skin. Thankful she had not decided to wear a red gown, Vanessa turned her attentions back to Miss Collins.

"Perhaps we should not judge Miss Plimpton so harshly." Miss Collins raised her perfectly shaped brows. "Indeed, there may be no one to advise her on what is proper and what is not. Certainly her mama would not know—she married a tradesman, after all."

Miss Waxter giggled again. "But that does not excuse Miss Plimpton's family from seeking advice on the matter. They certainly have the blunt to hire someone to advise them. Perhaps I shall ask Mama to suggest it to them."

"Indeed, I think it an excellent suggestion." Miss Collins nodded quickly. "We have a duty to alleviate this problem, you know. As part of the current group of debutantes, we shall be required to attend the same affairs as Miss Plimpton. If she continues to dress inappropriately, she will be an embarrassment to us all."

Miss Waxter smiled. "That is precisely what I fear, dear Honoria. I shall speak to Mama at the very next opportunity. Now let us put this unpleasant matter behind us, and speak of something more pleasant. What is your opinion of Miss Frothingale's gown? I think it quite elegant."

This remark prompted a discussion of the latest fashions and the advisability of donning various styles and hues. Vanessa's smile grew more strained with each moment that passed, but the group of chattering young ladies appeared not to notice. Not wishing to intrude upon their converse to take her leave, Vanessa simply smiled and inched her way to the edge of the group. Then she smoothly stepped back, appearing to respond to a summons from someone across the floor.

Gossip and gowns. Could anything be more boring? Vanessa joined a group of slightly older ladies. Perhaps their discussion would be more interesting. But their converse also consisted of fashions and the latest *on-dits*.

After leaving her fourth group, Vanessa gave up the attempt to socialize. It seemed there were no ladies at the ball who chose to discuss any other subjects. She was engaged in gazing at the dancers, attempting to catch a glimpse of Millie, when a gentleman approached her.

"Pardon me, Miss Holland." The pinched-faced young gentleman bowed slightly. "May I have the pleasure of this dance?"

Vanessa stared at him in shock for a moment, then responded as she had been taught. "Certainly, sir. I would be honored."

As she took his arm and he led her to the dance floor, Vanessa attempted to remember his name. Her papa had taught her a trick for recalling names, and she had used it in the reception line. His stiff and proper posture gave her the clue. He was March-something. Now she must recall the second half of his name.

While they were dancing, the bald spot upon the top of his head gave it away—Marchibald.

"I do hope you are enjoying the ball thus far, Mr. Marchibald." Vanessa smiled at him as the figures of the dance drew them within speaking distance.

"Yes, indeed." He preened slightly, appearing pleased she had remembered his name. "You are uncommonly tall for a female, Miss Holland."

"Yes, I suppose I am." Vanessa frowned slightly, wishing he had not mentioned the discrepancy in their heights. It made her even more aware she looked down at the top of his head.

"Must make it difficult. Most gentlemen like to look down upon a lady, you know?"

Vanessa bit back a sharp retort and kept the smile on her face. Mr. Marchibald had an air of superiority about him, and she had no doubt he often found himself looking down upon the females of the species.

"Makes it deuced hard to dance with you." Mr. Marchibald sighed loudly. "Take care you don't step on my toes, now. Don't fancy being crushed like a bug."

Vanessa's eyes widened at the insult, and she had all she could do not to reply in kind. Just in time, she managed to see the humor in the situation and merely nodded. Mr. Marchibald was a rude, conceited partner, but at least he *was* a partner.

"You do, however, appear to be quite agile for your size. What do you ride, Miss Holland?"

For a moment, Vanessa was nonplussed. Then she realized he was asking about horses, and her sense of humor took the upper hand. "Draft horses."

"You do not say!" Mr. Marchibald craned his head back to stare at her. "How did you find a sidesaddle that large?"

Vanessa smiled, gritting her teeth. There was little enjoyment in indulging her sense of humor when the recipient was too dull-witted to suspect she was telling a bouncer. "You must pardon me, Mr. Marchibald. I was making a small joke."

"A small joke, you say?" Mr. Marchibald snorted with laughter, an unattractive trait. "Nothing *small* about you."

At this point, the dance drew to a conclusion. Vanessa slipped into the crowd at the edge of the dance floor, thanking the gods the piece had not been longer. She had just gained an unobtrusive spot under a stand of potted greenery when another gentleman presented himself.

"There you are, Miss Holland. Would you care to dance?"

Vanessa smiled at the gentleman who stood before her and tried not to avert her head. The odor of strong spirits had accompanied him in the receiving line, and he had been introduced as a baron. He was dressed in black, as were all the gentlemen present, but he wore an unusually large gem on his elaborately arranged neckcloth. The gem was an amethyst, and it glittered in the lights from the chandeliers. It was the exact color of burgundy, and the moment she saw it, she knew his name. "I should be delighted, Lord Brandywine."

The dance was an ordeal, from the first step to the last. Lord Brandywine was much too occupied with nodding at acquaintances and catching the eye of pretty young ladies to attend to her. Indeed, he spoke not a word, and Vanessa was hard-pressed to keep the smile on her face. Why had he asked her to dance when he obviously wished to be elsewhere?

Breathing a sigh of relief, Vanessa regained her spot by the greenery. She was wondering whether she could politely refuse another dance if she were asked when an extremely young gentleman approached.

"Miss Holland? I say, would you . . . is . . . will you do me the . . . er . . . honor of dancing with . . . with me?"

Vanessa almost groaned. He was only a boy, no more than sixteen, if that. His cheeks still sported the roundness of youth and were bright pink with embarrassment. His complexion bore the marks of recent blemishes, and he gazed up at her with a pleading look in his eye, as if he hoped she might refuse.

"I should be honored." Vanessa repeated the familiar phrase, racking her brain to remember his name. He was just a lad and his face was marked. That was it. "Thank you, Mr. Ladmark."

His dancing was every bit as hesitant as his manner. Vanessa gamely suffered through the long measures, struggling to keep a smile on her face. Each time he made a misstep, Mr. Ladmark apologized most profusely, his words barely finished before he made the next blunder.

When Mr. Ladmark led her from the floor at last, Vanessa had no doubt he was every bit as relieved as she that their dance had concluded. He escorted her to her spot beneath the greenery and bowed slightly. "Thank you, Miss Holland, for a . . . a most enjoyable dance."

As Mr. Ladmark was walking away, Vanessa finally understood why three separate gentleman, each following upon the other's heels, had sought to partner her. Mr. Ladmark exchanged a speaking glance with Aunt Lolly, raising his brows as if to ask if he had been a good boy. Aunt Lolly nodded, favoring him with a smile in return.

Vanessa's face flamed. Aunt Lolly was dispatching gentlemen to dance with her, and that would not do at all. Vanessa turned quickly, neatly evading a fourth emissary from Aunt Lolly, and set off through the crowds to ask her to cease her efforts.

Ten

Vanessa's smile faltered a bit as she realized Stephen was at his mother-in-law's side. It was difficult to be close to him without giving away her feelings, but she must be circumspect.

"Hello, my dear." Aunt Lolly smiled as Vanessa approached. "Stephen and I were just commenting on how lovely you look."

A smile hovered at the corners of Stephen's mouth. "I daresay there isn't so much as a pony in sight."

"Thank you, Stephen." A blush rose to Vanessa's cheeks as she met his admiring gaze. She remembered the comment she'd made about how, as a debutante, she would be as noticeable as a horse in a field of cows. Aunt Lolly had said Stephen commented favorably on her gown. Vanessa had no doubt it was true, for Stephen's blue eyes sparkled with warmth as they surveyed her.

"Are you enjoying the evening?" Aunt Lolly seemed oblivious to the fond looks Stephen was casting in Vanessa's direction.

"I am, Aunt Lolly, but I must speak to you about the three gentlemen you have sent to partner me."

Aunt Lolly's eyes widened and she had the grace to look chagrined. "I am caught out, then?"

"You are." Vanessa smiled at Aunt Lolly's guilty expression. "I do appreciate your efforts, but, truly, I do not care to dance with unwilling partners."

Aunt Lolly sighed. "I thought I was being most circumspect about my arrangements. However did you tumble onto my machinations?"

"Mr. Marchibald approached me as if he were about to encounter a new breed of ferocious wild animal, Lord Brandywine failed to meet my eyes even once—it was obvious he wished he were elsewhere—and Mr. Ladmark apologized as if I were his schoolmaster."

"Their demeanor gave my game away?"

"That and Mr. Ladmark's actions. He exchanged a speaking glance with you the moment our dance concluded, as if he wanted praise for having discharged such an onerous duty."

"Oh, dear!" Aunt Lolly looked upset. "I did not intend to cause you any embarrassment."

A smile played around the corners of Vanessa's lips. "I am certain you did not. And I was not embarrassed. Instead, I attempted to solve the puzzle of why these gentlemen should seek me out for a dance. Pigs being led to slaughter offer more enthusiasm."

Aunt Lolly let out a peal of delighted laughter and then fanned her face frantically, attempting to mask her unladylike conduct. "Oh my, but you are refreshing, my dear! You are precisely as Stephen promised you would be."

Vanessa was not entirely certain Aunt Lolly's words were a compliment. "I am sorry if I have disappointed you."

"You did not disappoint me. The blame is mine for not choosing suitable partners for you. But you must understand I simply could not stand here doing nothing when you were not enjoying the evening."

"But I *was* enjoying the evening." Vanessa smiled to put the older woman at ease. "I joined several groups and listened to their converse, and I learned some things of interest about gossip and gowns from the young ladies who were not engaged in dancing."

"You did?" Aunt Lolly seemed a bit surprised.

"Yes, indeed. All gowns, no matter how fine, can be roundly criticized by those who do not favor the young ladies who are wearing them, and tongues will wag when they want, even when there is no provocation."

Stephen laughed. "I could have told you that, Vanessa. Did you learn anything else?"

"Yes. A reluctant partner is far worse than no partner at all."

"Then perhaps you should dance with a willing partner." Stephen smiled down at her. "Will you do me the honor of waltzing with me?"

Vanessa took a deep, steadying breath. How could she waltz with Stephen when his mama-in-law was watching? She longed to be in Stephen's arms, but Aunt Lolly might guess her feelings for him were not those of an employee or even of a friend. She had to think of some excuse for fear she might give all away.

"Vanessa?" Stephen was waiting for her answer.

Vanessa breathed a sigh of relief as she hit upon the perfect solution to her dilemma. "I know it seems absurd, Stephen, but convention does not allow me to waltz with you. I have not been given permission for the dance."

"You are correct, but there are solutions to every problem, and we shall fix it in a trice." Aunt Lolly turned to a lady who was standing nearby. "Sally dear, will you be so kind as to join us for a moment? We have a difficulty only you can solve."

The lady, who was wearing a lovely gold gown bedecked with jewels, joined their group. Vanessa's eyes widened as she remembered her from the reception line. It was Lady Sally Jersey, one of the patronesses at Almack's and an undisputed arbiter of society's conventions.

"No doubt you remember my dear son-in-law, Lord Bridgeford, and I believe you have made the acquaintance of my protégée, Miss Vanessa Holland."

"Of course. It is a pleasure to see you again, Lord Bridgeford." Lady Jersey smiled at Stephen, then turned to Vanessa. "And how could I forget the young lady who has received the nod from Her Majesty?"

Vanessa felt her cheeks turn pink with embarrassment. How had Lady Jersey found out about that? "Thank you, Lady Jersey, but I did nothing of consequence to gain Her Majesty's favor. I merely made a small suggestion."

"I daresay it was a bit more than that." Lady Jersey laughed. "Her Majesty has suffered from the headache for months and your *small suggestion* has relieved her of the ailment. I must admit I am curious about how you came by this knowledge of remedies."

Vanessa smiled. "From my father. He is in possession of all manner of remedies for common afflictions."

"Ah, yes, Baron Holland." Lady Jersey nodded. "I have heard he is a fine scholar and well respected among notable academics."

"Indeed, he is, Lady Jersey."

"Perhaps you would join me for tea, Miss Holland?" Lady Jersey smiled. "I should like to discuss a variety of subjects with you."

Vanessa's eyebrows shot up in surprise, but she quickly recovered. "I would be honored."

"Shall we say tomorrow at four?" Lady Jersey turned to Aunt Lolly. "I fear I have monopolized your Miss Holland, Lolly. You required my assistance?"

"Yes, indeed. Lord Bridgeford has requested Miss Holland partner him in a waltz, and she has correctly reminded us she has not yet received permission for the dance."

Lady Jersey smiled at Stephen. "I see no reason to withhold permission. Miss Holland's comportment is excellent, and she is clearly a levelheaded young miss. She has my approval to waltz with you, Lord Bridgeford."

"Thank you." Stephen looked properly grateful, but

Vanessa could see laughter lurking deep in his eyes as he turned to her. "I do believe they are about to play a waltz. Shall we remove ourselves to the dance floor?"

There was nothing for it but to smile and accept Stephen's arm. Vanessa took her leave of Lady Jersey and Aunt Lolly and gave a deep, resigned sigh as Stephen led her to the dance floor. She could not think of any other objection. She would waltz with him, but she would concentrate all her energies on the steps, pretending she was with the dancing master Aunt Lolly had hired. If she kept a polite smile on her face and a tight rein on her emotions, no aspect of her person would reveal her tender feelings for Stephen.

"What is wrong, Vanessa?" Stephen took her in his arms. "You look as if *you* are being led to slaughter."

Vanessa settled on the first excuse entered her mind. "I am concentrating, Stephen. I have never performed the waltz before, and I must count the measures so I will not make an error and tread upon your toes."

"The waltz is not so difficult as all that." Stephen grinned down at her. "And you must not worry about my toes. I have suffered through more than one Season and have become quite adept at avoiding that mishap."

"But I am regrettably unpracticed. I am apt to make several missteps, and I should not wish to injure you."

Stephen held her a bit closer and laughed. "I am certain you will not injure me. After all, I am a student of Gentleman Jackson, and I have learned all manner of fancy footwork from him."

"Gentleman Jackson?" The waltz began and Vanessa matched her steps with Stephen's, not even thinking about the forms of the dance. "How exciting that must be! I have heard of him and his remarkable skills. You must tell me all about your lessons. Perhaps you could even show me some of the things he has taught you."

"You wish to become a pugilist?"

At the laughter in Stephen's voice, Vanessa felt color rise to her cheeks. "No, of course not. But my curiosity is piqued. How does one avoid a blow?"

"One ducks." Stephen laughed out loud. "And if one fails to duck the blow in time, one is knocked flat on the mat. I'll show you when we are in private, if you truly are curious. But I must caution you it is not deemed seemly for a lady to discuss such elements of physicality with a gentleman."

"You forget I am not a lady." Vanessa smiled up at him sweetly.

"And *you* forget you are, by virtue of your father's new title and your presentation at court."

"You are right. I *did* forget. But does merely donning the trappings of a lady make me a lady?"

Stephen glanced down at her and an amused smile hovered on his lips. "I would say for all intents and purposes it does. You certainly look like a lady tonight, a very attractive lady. I would wager to say you are the most desirable lady here."

Vanessa did not reply. She *could* not reply. Her heart was singing too loudly and too happily. Stephen thought she was the most desirable lady at the ball. That pleased her more than anything else could.

"I must caution you." Stephen looked very serious. "Though Lolly and I appreciate your candor, you must refrain from sharing it with others. The *ton* does not look kindly upon such open honesty."

"You must not be concerned, Stephen. I shall guard my tongue when others are present. I promise I will limit myself to polite and dreadfully dull comments for the remainder of the evening."

"But not when you are alone with us." Stephen grinned. "It would be more than I could bear if your first venture into polite society killed the delightful minx in you."

Vanessa grinned back. "There is no danger of that. The only effective way to curb my tongue forever would be to truss me up like a Christmas goose and stuff chestnuts in my mouth."

Before Stephen could do more than give a startled gasp of laughter, the orchestra struck the final chords and the waltz concluded. Vanessa took Stephen's arm again and sighed, wishing their waltz could have continued a bit longer. It had been delightful to be in Stephen's strong arms, and she might never have that opportunity again.

"What is it?" Stephen stared at her with concern. "You look quite blue deviled."

Vanessa put on her brightest smile. "No, not in the slightest. I was simply comparing you to my other partners."

"And what were the results?"

"They came up wanting, of course." Vanessa felt heat rise to her cheeks again. She was blushing uncommonly much this evening. "Perhaps it is because you are taller than I am or that you are such an excellent partner. But when we danced, I felt dainty for the first time in my life."

Stephen smiled. "Thank you, Vanessa. And I felt as if I held Elgin's most lovely marble in my arms."

"You did?" Vanessa knew he intended his remark as a compliment, but she laughed softly. "I do hope I wasn't *that* unwieldy."

Stephen laughed. "That is not what I meant, and you know it!"

"Perhaps not." Vanessa laughed again, then let him lead her back to Aunt Lolly's side.

"You acquitted yourself well." Aunt Lolly gave her a nod of approval. "I watched you carefully and did not see Stephen wince even once."

Vanessa laughed, but she wondered exactly what Aunt Lolly had seen. Had she watched them carefully enough to guess Vanessa had fallen in love with her son-in-law?

"You have done your work well, Madame." Stephen winked at Aunt Lolly. "Vanessa dances very well, indeed, and her conversation is most charming. I daresay you will succeed in making a proper lady out of her before the Season is over."

Aunt Lolly smiled. "Perhaps I shall. But not *too* proper, I hope. Vanessa is like a breath of fresh air, and I am most hesitant about closing the window."

"Still, one must be careful not to catch a chill." Vanessa felt gratified as Aunt Lolly's lips twitched up at the corners. "Is there any way I may help you, Aunt Lolly, now Millie is getting along so famously on her own?"

"Help me?" Aunt Lolly looked puzzled. "With what, my dear?"

Vanessa sighed. She hoped Aunt Lolly would not think she was too forthcoming, but there was something she had been wishing to say. "I have noticed you are in the habit of excusing yourself at this hour of the evening to go to your husband's quarters. I thought perhaps I could assist you."

"You are extremely observant." Aunt Lolly looked a bit discomfited, but then she smiled. "Perhaps there is something that you could do, my dear. I should like you to accompany me to my husband's quarters, if you would care to do so. Charles shuns most visitors, so you must not be upset if he chooses not to speak with you, but . . ."

"But what, Aunt Lolly?"

"It has suddenly occurred to me that dear Charles has been shut off from all society for the past several years. Though he has never complained, he must be thoroughly bored speaking only to Stephen and to me. Perhaps Charles might also enjoy a breath of fresh air."

Eleven

Aunt Lolly waited until they had left the ballroom to turn to Vanessa. "I must prepare you for your meeting with Charles."

"Please do, Aunt Lolly. I know he is ill; Stephen explained that before we accepted your kind invitation. But he did not give us the particulars. From what ailment does Lord Treverton suffer?"

"The doctors are not certain." Aunt Lolly frowned. "Or if they are, they have not seen fit to tell me. But you must prepare yourself for a bit of a shock. My husband's illness has taken a dreadful toll."

"In what manner?"

Aunt Lolly sighed, and it was clear she was reluctant to discuss the subject. "Charles has lost partial use of his left leg and arm and the left side of his face is . . . is disfigured. It is why he does not receive visitors. My husband is proud, and he does not wish others to see him in his present state."

"I see." Vanessa was pleased Aunt Lolly trusted her, and she took the older woman's arm in an effort to reassure her. "You must not be concerned over my reaction. I have seen all manner of illness in my work with Papa."

"Then you will not be disgusted by Charles's appearance?"

"Not in the slightest." Vanessa shook her head. "Has

Lord Treverton suffered any diminishment of his intellect?"

Aunt Lolly turned to her in surprise. "No, indeed not! Charles is every bit as discerning as he was before his illness."

"That is excellent, Aunt Lolly. I have seen others who were not so fortunate. Is it difficult for Lord Treverton to speak?"

"It was a struggle for him at first, but he has made great improvement of late. I am certain you will be able to understand his words."

Vanessa nodded, filing this bit of information away in her mind. If Lord Treverton was improving now, there was hope he might improve even more with the proper therapy. "You must not be anxious. I am certain I will enjoy meeting Lord Treverton immensely."

"I do hope you will." Aunt Lolly breathed an audible sigh of relief. "I cannot help but believe Charles will be amused by your outspoken comments and your candor. He has been in a brown study of late, and I am hopeful you will lift his spirits."

"I will do my best." Vanessa smiled as they approached the end of the hallway and Aunt Lolly tapped lightly on the door to her husband's chambers.

An older woman opened the door. She smiled at Aunt Lolly and moved aside so they could enter.

"I should like you to meet Camilla Barrow, Vanessa. She is an excellent nurse, as well as a distant cousin, and she is in charge when I am unable to be at my husband's side." Aunt Lolly turned to the nurse. "This is Miss Vanessa Holland, Camilla. How is Charles faring this evening?"

"Very well, Lolly. He told me he was eagerly anticipating seeing you in your new ball gown. But I have not prepared him for the fact he has a visitor."

"How could you, Camilla? I did not know I would ask

Vanessa to accompany me." Aunt Lolly turned to Vanessa. "Will you wait here with Camilla while I tell Charles you have come to visit him?"

"Certainly."

When Aunt Lolly had left the outer chamber, Camilla turned to Vanessa. "Has she prepared you for seeing Charles?"

"Yes." Vanessa smiled. "And neither you nor Aunt Lolly need be anxious, as I have encountered others with the same affliction. Is Lord Treverson's left side completely paralyzed?"

Camilla looked shocked for a moment at the bluntness of the question, but then she shook her head. "He cannot move his left leg without assistance, but his left arm has regained some of its strength. He is now able to close his fingers around an object."

"Before the onset of his illness, did Lord Treverton favor his left hand, or his right?"

"His right. Charles has always held the pen in his right hand. And his fork, also."

"I am glad to hear that," Vanessa said. "Then he can still put pen to paper and use utensils without aid?"

"Yes, indeed."

"You must tell me about his face, Camilla. When Lord Treverton smiles, does the left side of his mouth turn upward?"

"No, it does not."

"And his left eyelid. Does it droop slightly?"

"Yes!" Camilla looked thoroughly astonished. "How did you know this without ever setting eyes on him?"

"The symptoms are quite common, and my father's older brother suffered the same ailment. That is why I told you there was no need for you to be anxious. I have encountered this particular illness before."

Camilla leaned forward eagerly. "Tell me about your uncle. How did he fare?"

"Quite well, actually." Vanessa smiled. "My father de-signed several devices to assist him. By using them, he was able to lead a normal life. Perhaps they would also be of use to Lord Treverton. If he is receptive, I shall mention them."

The door to Lord Treverton's bedchamber opened and Aunt Lolly came out. "Vanessa? Charles has agreed to see you."

Vanessa crossed the room with a smile on her face and entered Lord Treverton's bedchamber. The once-hand-some man, who was sitting up on his bed, was indeed disfigured. The left side of his face was slack, and it was clear his left leg was useless to him. He did not look happy to see her, but Vanessa had expected that from what little Aunt Lolly had told her. She crossed the room and delib-erately took his right hand. "Lord Treverton. This is a pleasure. I thank you for your hospitality. Both Millie and I are most grateful for your kindness to us."

"S'only right we take you in." Lord Treverton's words were slightly slurred, but Vanessa had no difficulty in un-derstanding him. "You have great height, Miss Holland."

"Vanessa. I wish you had been in the ballroom to see me dancing with Mr. Ladmark. It was a most amusing pair-ing, quite like a horse attempting to waltz with a chick."

Lord Treverton's lips turned up on the right side and he gave a startled laugh. "You don't say! A horse with a chick?"

"Did you know Mr. Marchibald is beginning to lose his hair? I saw it quite clearly from my height. His valet brushes it to the side, to attempt to cover the exposed scalp, but his pate gleamed like a beacon in the lights of the chandelier."

Lord Treverton laughed again and used his right hand to pat the bed next to him. "S'down, my dear, and tell me more."

"Mr. Marchibald seemed very anxious I might step on

his toes." Vanessa sat down on the edge of the bed and smiled at Lord Treverton. "He feared I might quash him like a bug."

Lord Treverton frowned, lopsidedly. "He told you that?"

"He did, and I must admit I harbored the desire to do just that." Vanessa lifted her skirt and showed Lord Treverton her dancing slippers. "But these are new dancing slippers and I did not wish to ruin them."

"You do not strike me as the type of young miss who would accept such an insult with a smile. What *did* you do?"

Vanessa laughed. "You are quite right in your assessment of my character, Lord Treverton. I enjoyed bamming Mr. Marchibald a bit."

"How?"

Lord Treverton grinned. He seemed not to care that his lips curved up lopsidedly, and Vanessa was glad. She'd made him forget about his affliction for the moment. "He asked me if I rode. I told him that my favorite mount was a draft horse."

"A draft horse?"

"Precisely. And he believed me. He even queried me about where I obtained a sidesaddle that large!"

Lord Treverton burst into laughter again, but he quickly sobered. "I apologize. I should not be laughing at Mr. Marchibald's regrettably rude behavior."

"But why should you not? It is funny." Vanessa grinned at him. "I should never have survived twenty-six years with my height and weight if I had not developed an uncommonly good sense of humor."

Lord Treverton nodded. "Yes, there is that. Perhaps I should develop more humor regarding my condition. It appears to be of great benefit to you, and you do not appear to be unhappy."

"I am not." Vanessa smiled. "Dear Papa told me we

may change some aspects of our appearance, and there is no benefit in dwelling on those we cannot."

Lord Treverton looked thoughtful. "Your papa is a wise man. Tell me more about your dancing partners. It is good to laugh."

"Lord Brandywine also favored me with his attentions—though I am not certain it was a favor." Vanessa took Lord Treverton's left hand and noticed with pleasure his fingers closed around hers. "I felt quite light-headed by the time our dance was concluded."

"Why's that?"

"The fumes, of course. I suspect he is a hopeless tosspot and a rogue."

"A rogue?" Lord Treverton raised his eyebrows, the right much higher than the left. "Brandywine?"

"Indeed. I suspect he has focused his attentions on Lady Cecilia Dartley."

"You do not say." Lord Treverton gripped her hand a little more tightly. "Why, Vanessa?"

Vanessa noted, with pleasure, he had made use of her Christian name. She leaned a little closer so her lips were near his ear. "I should not spread tales, Lord Treverton. Promise me you will not repeat what I am about to say."

"I promise. You must call me Charles. If we are to share *on-dits* together, it is ridiculous to stand on formality."

Vanessa nodded. "You are right. While I was partnering Lord Brandywine, I noticed he expended great effort to join the set Lady Dartley and her partner were forming. And when the figures of the dance brought her into his arms, his hand brushed a portion of her anatomy no disinterested lady would allow."

"If that is the way the wind blows, Brandywine had best take all caution. Lord Dartley is an uncommonly good shot."

Vanessa laughed. "It is possible I am wrong, but I do not believe so. As Lord Brandywine took Lady Dartley into his arms, the expression on his face reminded me of Squire Pearson's prize cow."

"Squire Pearson's cow?" Lord Treverton called out to his wife. "Come and join us, Lolly. Sit here on the bed. Vanessa is about to tell us of Squire Pearson's prize cow."

Aunt Lolly exchanged a speaking glance with Vanessa, one filled with happiness and gratitude. And then she came to sit on the bed, taking her husband's other hand. "Of course, my darling. Tell us more, Vanessa."

"It happened last spring, when the squire's cow became locked in the grain bin by mistake. The error was discovered quite soon, before any real damage was done, but I happened to be there when the squire went to let her out. She was standing there, munching happily, as if she were the honored guest at a sumptuous bovine banquet."

Stephen stood in the doorway, smiling at the threesome on the bed. Lord Treverton's color was high, and he appeared to be thoroughly enjoying himself. Indeed, Stephen had not seen him so contented since before his illness, and there was good reason for his contentment. Charles was the sole interest of two lovely ladies, and both were holding his hands.

For a moment, Stephen found himself wishing he were in his papa-in-law's position. He should like nothing more than to recline on his bed, and hold Vanessa's hand. But the thought of Vanessa sitting on the edge of his bed brought forth other images, images he immediately forced from his mind. Though the thought was not a happy one, he must not forget he was lawfully wedded to Lord Treverton's daughter.

Stephen concentrated on their converse for a moment and listened to their lighthearted word play. It should not surprise him Vanessa was so candid and natural with his papa-in-law. It was her nature to be so. He had expected

they would rub along well together, and he was not disappointed.

As he watched, Lord Treverton chuckled and then
broke into a full laugh. Stephen had not heard his papa-
in-law laugh since he had been struck down by his illness.
There was no doubt Vanessa's presence was excellent therapy for him. He had been correct in bringing her to London.

Stephen smiled. It had not only been the correct thing
to do—it had been the most expedient. He had not
wanted to be separated from Vanessa for the entire Season. The months he absented himself from Bridgeford
Hall were difficult enough to endure, but they were necessary. Stephen had borne them with as much good grace
as he had been able to muster. Still, he had discovered
any time he spent away from Vanessa made him long for
her even more.

Did he love her? Stephen frowned. He was quite certain
he did, but he must not speak of his love. He did not have
leave to court her or to invite her fond feelings toward
him. To encourage Vanessa to regard him as more than
a friend would be a disservice to her.

It had been agony to hold her in his arms and waltz
with her. Even though he had kept up the polite banter
between them, he'd found himself wanting to draw her
closer, to feel her delightful body against his. Of course,
he had not acted upon his desire. He had vowed to be
circumspect in his dealings with Vanessa, and he would
not break that vow.

"It is time for your draft, Charles." Camilla stepped
into the bedchamber with a tray.

"Already?" Charles turned to her in amazement. "But
it seems as if only moments have passed since Vanessa
came to visit me."

Aunt Lolly laughed. "It has been the better part of an
hour, dear. It is now approaching eleven."

Stephen watched as Aunt Lolly took the cup from the tray and held it to her husband's lips. It was difficult for Charles to drink, and some of the liquid escaped his lips and dripped onto the counterpane.

"Excuse me, Aunt Lolly." Vanessa moved forward and took the cup. "I believe I could be of some assistance."

"How?" Aunt Lolly stared at her in confusion.

"I have just remembered a device Papa made to help my uncle drink. He had the same affliction, you see, and he could not drink in the normal manner."

"What is it, Vanessa?" Charles asked, interested. "I have done my best, but I cannot hold my lip tightly against the rim of the cup."

Vanessa nodded. "Papa's device might be of use. If one of the servants will cut several reeds from your lily pond and bring me a sharp knife so I may trim them properly, I will show you how the device is used."

"I'll fetch the reeds, if you would care to try it." Stephen stepped into the room. "And a sharp knife from the kitchens, as well."

Charles nodded, smiling at him. "Hello, Stephen. You are here just in time to be of use. Please do fetch the reeds Vanessa has requested. I am weary of drooling when I attempt to drink, and I shall be delighted to try any device that will alleviate that embarrassment."

Stephen hurried down the stairs and into the kitchens, surprising Lord Treverton's staff with his request for the sharpest knife they possessed. He cut several reeds at the lily pond and was back in his papa-in-law's chambers before five minutes had passed.

"Will these do?" Stephen held out the reeds and the knife for her approval.

"Splendidly." Vanessa smiled at him. Then she turned to her work, plying the knife expertly and cutting the reeds to the correct size. Once she had finished, she turned to Lord Treverton with a smile. "You have indulged in cigars, have you not?"

Lord Treverton looked surprised. "Indeed, I have. Why?"

"It is the same theory. You must stick the reed into your cup and draw on it the way you would a cigar. The liquid will rise in the reed and flow into your mouth, and you need only use the right side of your mouth if the left side refuses to cooperate."

"I see." Lord Treverton nodded. "Let me attempt it, and we will discover whether your clever suggestion will work."

Stephen watched as Charles drew on the reed. It worked like a charm, and his cup was drained in short order without spilling a drop of the medication.

"Ingenious!" Lord Treverton nodded, well pleased. "I shall order several dozen reeds cut of this very size and shape. You are kind to tell me of this invention."

Vanessa smiled. "There are several more inventions my father devised in caring for my uncle. Some of them improved his condition quite dramatically. If you are agreeable, I will visit you tomorrow to tell you about them."

"I am certainly agreeable." Charles smiled at her. "In fact, I am eager to hear anything you should care to tell me."

"Good. Then I will leave you now, so you may bid Aunt Lolly good night in privacy. Until tomorrow, Charles."

Vanessa leaned close and placed a kiss on Charles's cheek. Charles reached up to pat her arm and Stephen smiled with pleasure. Vanessa would do much good in this sad household, of that he was certain. She had already succeeded in lifting his papa-in-law's spirits more than any of them had in the past.

"Good night, Charles." Stephen walked over to clasp his papa-in-law's right hand. "I shall take my leave now and accompany Vanessa back to the ball."

Charles nodded. "Yes, you do that. She is a delight, Stephen, and I am grateful to you for bringing her here. It seems rather odd to say so, as I have only just met Vanessa, but I must confess I feel she is part of our family."

"Vanessa has that effect upon people." Stephen left the bedchamber with a heart much lightened. Charles had experienced the same reaction to Vanessa that Millie had enjoyed. His sister had also regarded Vanessa as a friend immediately following their first meeting, and there was no doubt Millie considered her a part of their family.

He spotted Vanessa at the end of the hallway about to descend the staircase. "If you will wait a moment, I will escort you back to the ballroom."

Vanessa stopped and waited for him. When he joined her, she smiled happily. "Charles is simply marvelous, Stephen. I am so happy I have met him at last!"

"He is equally happy." Stephen took her arm. "I have never seen him so delighted with a visitor before. I am most impressed with your kindness to a gentleman you have just met."

"But, truly, I feel as if I have known him longer. And he needs me. I cared for my uncle and I know a bit about this ailment. It is extremely frustrating to be a prisoner of one's body."

"It must be." Stephen guided her carefully down the stairs as if he were escorting a precious being he wished to protect from harm. "I have no doubt there is much Charles desires to do and is unable to accomplish."

Vanessa nodded. "We must help him become more independent. Charles is willing to attempt something new. He did not object when I taught him to use the reed, and I do believe Papa's inventions and therapies can be of great benefit to him."

"Does that mean you will take on the task of helping him?"

"Of course I will." Vanessa turned to smile up at him.

"And it is not a task. It will provide great pleasure for us both."

Stephen smiled back at her, his heart bursting with pride. Vanessa truly wished to help Charles, and he had no doubt she would. She was wonderfully kind and compassionate. Most young ladies would have balked at spending hours in the sickroom, preferring to avail themselves of all the entertainments the Season had to offer. But Vanessa was different. She possessed every one of the qualities he admired. He grasped her arm a little more tightly and wished with all his heart he had married Vanessa instead of the vain, selfish, fluff-headed lady who was his countess.

Twelve

"You must not fuss so, Colette." Vanessa smiled at the abigail, who was attempting to brush her hair. "I do not expect any morning callers and am quite presentable, under the circumstances."

Colette shook her head as she put down the silver-backed brush. "Your hair, it is impossible this day. It has more tangles than strands! And even though I attempted to dry it, it is still damp. Whatever did you do to make your hair so?"

"I had a slight mishap while I assisted Lord Treverton during his exercises in the pool. I am not precisely certain how, but I tumbled in and had a good dunking. Have I truly made a mess of my hair?"

"Indeed. It is so thick and tangled I cannot pull the brush through it. I admit defeat. Your hair, it is quite impossible for me to arrange."

Vanessa glanced at her reflection. Her long, thick hair resembled nothing so much as a briar patch. "This simply will not do. You have been brushing my hair for over a half hour, and it is still a jumble. You have wasted your talents, and I must make your work easier."

"If only you could." Colette sighed. "But how?"

Vanessa began to smile. "I could cut it off short. Then my hair will not hinder my therapy with Lord Treverton and will take less time for you to brush."

"*Merci*!" Colette rolled her eyes to the ceiling. "You

must not say such things, even in jest. Your hair, it is lovely when it is brushed, and the current style would not allow for such a thing. All the young ladies have lengthy hair this Season."

"But if it were shorter, it would make my toilette much easier, would it not?"

"Of course. But you will be unfashionable."

"Bother fashion!" Vanessa waved that concern away. "Short hair or long, I will still be unfashionable. A goose dressed as a swan is still a goose."

"Miss Vanessa!"

Colette was clearly shocked, and Vanessa grinned at her. "There is nothing to discuss. I have decided to cut my hair, and I will wield the shears myself if you will not."

"But are you certain this is proper?"

"I am," Vanessa stated. "Unfortunately, I am not practiced at cutting hair. I should think you would make better work of it than I would. Fetch the scissors and let us shear off these horrid tangles."

Colette looked as if she wanted to refuse, but the determined look on Vanessa's face convinced her. "You are determined to cut it if I will not?"

"Yes, indeed. My hair has always been unruly. I should have shorn it long ago."

"Then I will do it," Colette said. "I would not like to see you make the attempt. You are far too impulsive and you may wind up without a hair left on your head."

Colette fetched the shears, and Vanessa smiled as she leaned back in the chair. "Do as you wish, Colette. There are many enjoyable pastimes in this life, and sitting here for almost an hour while you brush out the tangles in my hair is not among them."

"I agree." Colette gave a little nod. "Perhaps if I shape it longer in the back, we shall still have the use of the clasp."

"Good. I should not like to be without it. Do not stand

on ceremony. Wield the shears and free me from this un-welcome burden."

As Colette began to snip with the shears, Vanessa closed her eyes and thought about Charles. He was making extraordinary progress, just as she had hoped he would. Papa had sent detailed instructions for the exercises he deemed most helpful, and Vanessa had begun to teach them to Charles and Aunt Lolly's cousin, Camilla. Though only two weeks had passed, Charles's left arm was much stronger and he was able to gesture and lift light objects. His left leg was improving also, though it might never regain full strength.

Charles had been most surprised when Vanessa had asked him for permission to convert the apartment next to his quarters into an exercise room. He had agreed, and Vanessa had quickly commissioned an indoor pool built very much like the lily pond, though not as large. It was made of thin metal and sat on a metal carriage with wheels. A brazier, which was placed under the center of the pool, heated the water inside.

Though the water had to be carried up the stairs to Lord Treverton's bedchamber, the servants were eager to do so, forming a human chain and passing up buckets to fill the device. Unlike a hip bath, it did not have to be emptied with the use of buckets. Vanessa's Papa had de-vised a unique system for draining the device. It was wheeled to the window, cranked up to the proper height by a series of strong pulleys, and dumped unceremoni-ously into the kitchen herb garden. It was this pool into which Vanessa had fallen, giggling like a schoolgirl as she lost her balance and causing Charles to snort with laugh-ter at her dunking.

But Charles's returning strength was not the only bene-fit from the therapy. His outlook on life had changed as well. He permitted Vanessa to commission a Bath chair, and he now spent several hours in his study each afternoon. He was gradually resuming control of his money and his lands from those hired to fill the gap in his absence, and Vanessa suspected the fact he felt useful again was at the root of his new happiness.

The day after meeting Charles for the first time, Vanessa had embarked upon an exhausting schedule, but one that gave her much pleasure. She began her day by spending an hour with Charles, regaling him with humorous stories of the evening she had spent and supervising his exercises. She then dressed in suitable attire and joined Aunt Lolly and Millie as they entertained callers in the drawing room or paid calls upon others of their acquaintance.

In the late afternoon, when they returned, Vanessa went to Charles's chambers to take tea with him. After tea, it was time to dress for the evening's entertainment, join Aunt Lolly and Millie for a light repast, and go off to the theater or a ball or a dinner party.

Though none could deny Charles was improving, there was one aspect of his life Vanessa had been unable to change. He still refused to receive visitors, insisting no one see him in his weakened condition. Vanessa hoped Charles's stubborn refusal to socialize would change eventually, but for the present, he was firm in his intentions.

Surprisingly, Vanessa found she had been accepted by the *ton.* She had no doubt word of her kindness to Lord Treverton had spread, as she had overheard Aunt Lolly mentioning it to several of her friends. When asked by others, Vanessa took care not to provide any information regarding Charles's condition. Instead, she referred queries to Aunt Lolly, saying she did not wish to speak out of turn.

Though Vanessa was well liked by the debutantes and the young gentleman alike, she had no suitors. This was not in the least disappointing, as she had not expected to attract any notice of that nature. Millie, however, had two

suitors. One was John, Lord Holmsby, a shy young vis-
count who had recently inherited his father's title, and
Vanessa liked him immensely. The other was Mr. Durwin
Woodhouse, the third son of a baron, and Vanessa did
not care for him at all.

Lord Holmsby was intelligent and kind, the sort of
young gentleman who saw past Millie's wealth, revered
her good qualities, and would be an excellent husband.
He was handsome, possessed a good sense of humor, and
was well liked by the other gentlemen and ladies of the
ton. Mr. Woodhouse, however, was a horse of another
color, and Vanessa was most uneasy about his attentions
to Millie.

Mr. Woodhouse was a pink of the *ton.* There was no
other way to phrase it. He was handsome, his manners
were impeccable, and he dressed in the height of fashion.
But Vanessa suspected he had no more substance than a
puff of smoke, and she hoped Millie would not be taken
in by his town bronze and his lavish compliments. Vanessa
was not entirely certain Mr. Woodhouse was a civet in the
guise of a parlor cat, but she had vowed to watch him
carefully for the slightest indication he was attempting to
hide his true nature. She had her doubts Mr. Woodhouse
was sincere in the affection he claimed to have for Millie,
but, as yet, she had been unable to prove her suspicions.

"Miss Vanessa? It is finished!"

Colette's exclamation brought Vanessa from her reverie
and she opened her eyes. The sight made her gasp and
then smile with delight at her reflection. Colette had cut
her hair so short that she resembled a shorn lamb. The
feathery curls lay like a shining blond cap around her face
and angled back to form a cascade at the base of her
neck.

"Are you pleased?"

Colette sounded anxious, and Vanessa smiled to reassure her. "It is lovely! However did you curl it so nicely?"

"I did not curl it at all." Colette seemed well pleased with herself. "Once I cut off the length and your hair had less weight, what remained sprang up into curls, all by itself."

Vanessa nodded, reaching up to fluff her soft, curly hair. "Does this mean you will not be required to curl it?"

"It does! All I need do is smooth it with the brush and it will curl of its own accord. And brushing it also will be much easier now it has no great length."

"You are a genius, Colette."

"But I have done nothing." Colette waved the compliment away. "And though I feared it would not be so, I am of the opinion your hair is even more beautiful in this new style."

Vanessa wondered what her secret admirer would say if he saw her with her shorn hair. In his letters to her, he had complimented the color and the length of her hair, comparing it to long shafts of sunlight. Would he be disappointed she had cut it?

"Vanessa? Whatever is taking you so long to get . . . " Millie stopped short at the sight of Vanessa's new coiffure. Her mouth was still open and she gasped slightly, seemingly incapable of continuing her speech.

"Colette cut it for me." Vanessa smiled. "Do come in and see if you approve."

Millie moved into the room and stood before Vanessa, gazing at her hair critically. Then she smiled and nodded. "I *do* like it. It's very different from the current style, but somehow it suits you. Come along with me and we will see how Woody likes it. He has promised to call today."

"Woody?" Vanessa picked up her fan and her gloves and hurried off to join Millie.

"Mr. Woodhouse. He has asked me to call him *Woody*, as Mr. Woodhouse is so long and difficult to say."

"You must not, Millie," Vanessa cautioned her as they went down the stairs. "Addressing him as *Woody* would amount to the same as using his Christian name, and a young lady cannot do that unless she is engaged."

"You are right. I simply forgot. And he has not declared for me as yet."

"Do you expect him to?" Vanessa held her breath, waiting for Millie to answer.

"I do believe he will, eventually. He seems quite enamored of me."

"And are you enamored of him?"

"I am not certain. I shall have to wait and see. I also like Lord Holmsby, though he is not as fashionable or as exciting. I do not have to choose quite yet, do I, Vanessa?"

"Most certainly not!" Vanessa breathed a sigh of relief to learn Millie was not firmly smitten. "You do not have to choose until the conclusion of the Season, and not even then, if you do not care to do so."

Millie smiled. "Good. I am having too much fun to settle down with one gentleman. I must first fall in love, and then we shall see."

"Yes, indeed."

"Whom do you prefer? Mr. Woodhouse or Lord Holmsby?"

"I prefer Lord Holmsby."

"But why?" Millie looked puzzled. "He is really quite ordinary compared to Mr. Woodhouse."

"Perhaps, but I think he is kind and wise and good. I also think that he would make an excellent and loving husband."

"You may very well be right." Millie smiled. "But Mr. Woodhouse is so exciting. I am not certain I could give him up to marry Lord Holmsby."

"That is a question you must decide, Millie, for you will be the one to live with the result of your decision. But I should think Mr. Woodhouse's exciting nature might wear thin after a few years of marriage. At the same time, I doubt the steadfast love of a gentleman like Lord Holmsby could ever grow dim."

"You have made an excellent point." Millie nodded quickly. "I shall think about what you have said."

Vanessa closed her lips and kept them closed, even though she wanted to warn Millie not to settle her affections upon Mr. Woodhouse. She had given her opinion. Further discussion might make Millie determined to defend Mr. Woodhouse and choose him over Lord Holmsby.

The last of their callers had departed and Aunt Lolly, Millie, and Vanessa were in the drawing room, relaxing after having discharged their social obligations. Vanessa reached up to fluff her short hair and turned to Aunt Lolly. "Have I made a dreadful error in instructing Colette to cut my hair?"

"I am certain you have not." Aunt Lolly smiled. "I must admit I was shocked when I first set eyes on you, but the more I see of your new coiffure, the more I think it suits you."

"I have come to like it, also," Millie said. "And Mr. Woodhouse praised it lavishly. I do believe you have begun a new trend. Miss Parker confided to me that she had always desired to cut her hair, but did not have the courage to do so. Perhaps by this time tomorrow, several other debutantes will have copied your actions."

"Do you really think so?" Vanessa laughed as Millie nodded. "I had never thought to be in the first stare of fashion, Millie. I am not certain it pleases me."

Aunt Lolly smiled at her two charges. "I have long known that fashion is fickle, my dears. A lady may attempt to follow the current fashion, but it changes so rapidly the effort is nearly impossible. I think it best each lady dress in her most becoming manner and leave it at that."

"Hodges thought I might find you here." Stephen entered the drawing room and crossed the floor to place a kiss on Aunt Lolly's cheek. "I have just come from your husband's study and he requested I find you immediately."

An expression of anxiety crossed Aunt Lolly's face. "Is something wrong, Stephen? Does Charles wish me to come to him?"

"Nothing is wrong, and I apologize if I gave you that impression. Charles had a suggestion he wished me to discuss with the three of you."

"What is it?" Vanessa leaned forward.

"Good heavens!" Stephen stepped closer and stared at her with amazement. "What have you done to your hair?"

"I asked Colette to cut it off. It was far too long to brush every day. Do you approve?"

"Why . . . I . . . " Stephen appeared at a loss for words. "I am not certain. I am used to viewing you with lovely long hair, and now it has vanished."

"It has not vanished, Stephen. It is still in my room, unless Colette has already swept it up and placed it in the dustbin." Vanessa rose from her chair and twirled slowly around, fluffing her short curls with her fingers. When she came round to face Stephen again, she saw he was smiling and she breathed a sigh of relief. "You like it, then?"

"Yes, I believe I do. It somehow . . ."

Stephen paused, struggling for the correct phrase, and Aunt Lolly was quick to provide it. "Suits her?"

"Precisely. It suits you, Vanessa. But I shall miss the long strands of sunlight that fell past your shoulders."

Vanessa took her seat again, her breath catching in her throat. Stephen's words mirrored the ones her secret admirer had written. Did all gentlemen think her hair resembled sunlight?

"You said Charles had a suggestion for us?" Aunt Lolly poured Stephen a cup of tea and passed it to him.

"Indeed, he did. He thought you might enjoy hosting a Valentine's Day Ball, a romantical evening of dining and dancing for everyone who has arrived in London for the Season. He even had a few suggestions for decorating the ballroom for the event, and he wishes to discuss them with you in detail. He realizes that the time is short, and he wishes to be of assistance. He also mentioned he first met you at a Valentine's Day Ball."

Aunt Lolly beamed at Stephen. "We did meet at a Valentine's Day Ball. It was unusual, as few celebrate the holiday, but I do remember each lady drew a gentleman's name and wrote several lines of poetry to him—anonymously, of course. The gentlemen did the same for the ladies, and it was quite amusing to speculate on who had written to whom."

"Did Uncle Charles write a poem to you, Aunt Lolly?" Millie's eyes were shining.

The color rose to Aunt Lolly's cheeks. "Indeed, and I have kept his verse all these years."

"And his sentiments still have the power to put you to the blush!" Stephen laughed, reaching out to take Aunt Lolly's hand. "Did you also write a poem to him?"

"No, I drew another gentleman's name. I do not recall who he was. I wrote something regrettably insipid, for I am not a poetess."

Millie's eyes began to sparkle. "Could we write verses for our Valentine's Day Ball, Aunt Lolly?"

"No, dear, our guest list will be far too extensive for that. But I do not see why we cannot revive some of the old customs from other Valentine celebrations. You girls must help me research those."

Millie nodded eagerly. "Of course we shall, Aunt Lolly. I am so happy Uncle Charles is taking an interest in these things once again. It must mean his health is improving."

"I daresay it does." Aunt Lolly looked over at Vanessa

and exchanged a speaking glance. "I shall go to him now and discuss our plans for the event."

Vanessa smiled, keeping her own counsel as Aunt Lolly rushed off to see her husband. Just this morning, she had mentioned St. Valentine's Day was approaching in two weeks' time, and Charles had confided it was the anniversary of his first meeting with Aunt Lolly. Since Charles was improving both in mind and in body, perhaps he had decided he was ready to take his place as Aunt Lolly's husband once more. If so, Vanessa was delighted. She felt a bit like the legendary Cupid.

"Let us go up to our chambers to see what we shall wear to the ball." Millie jumped to her feet and smiled at Vanessa. "Hurry, Vanessa. If we decide to order new gowns, we must do so immediately."

Stephen placed his hand on Vanessa's arm. "You go ahead, Millie. I wish to speak with Vanessa for a moment on a matter of some importance."

Vanessa waited until Millie had left the chamber to turn to Stephen. "What is it, Stephen?"

"Let us walk in the garden. I prefer not to discuss the matter here."

"Of course." Vanessa rose to her feet, suddenly anxious. Stephen looked overset, and she hoped it was not a serious matter. She accepted his arm and walked with him out of the drawing room, wondering how she could possibly manage to react with pleasure if he told her his wife was well and would soon join them in London.

Thirteen

Vanessa trembled as she stepped into the gardens with Stephen. The comfort of his arm was reassuring, but he had not spoken since they left the drawing room. Wishing to break the tension, Vanessa attempted to read his expression. "I know you are disturbed over something. What is amiss?"

"In a moment." Stephen led her down a winding path to Aunt Lolly's lily pond, where they sat on one of the stone benches. "You must promise to save me two waltzes at the Valentine's Day Ball."

Vanessa felt the heat rise to her cheeks at the thought of being in Stephen's arms. She had been dreaming of waltzing with him again, but she knew it was dangerous to do so. No one must know of her tender feelings toward this handsome, compelling, and very married gentleman.

"Shall we say the first waltz and the last?" Stephen smiled down at her, but his eyes were clouded with worry.

Vanessa hesitated. She knew she should not promise, but she could not resist. "Yes, I shall save those dances for you. And now will you please tell me what is wrong?"

"Woodhouse."

"I should have known!" Vanessa let out a deep sigh of relief. "I, too, have my doubts about Mr. Woodhouse."

Stephen's blue eyes were solemn. "He has been a frequent caller of late, and Lolly told me he appears enamored of Millie."

"He has sent flowers to Millie every day and has partnered her at all the parties we have attended," Vanessa said. "It appears to be much more than a casual interest."

"What is your opinion of him?"

"I have reserved judgment for the time being. I have been watching Mr. Woodhouse carefully, Stephen, but I can find nothing truly objectionable. All the same, something about him is not quite right. I have no real basis for my suspicion, but I cannot completely trust him."

Stephen nodded, the ghost of a smile hovering round his lips. "We think alike in that, Vanessa. I do not trust him, either. You must tell me how Millie regards him. Is she agreeable toward Woodhouse's advances?"

"I fear she is. She admitted this morning she harbors affection for him. But she harbors a like affection for Lord Holmsby."

"Lord Holmsby?" Stephen looked surprised, but nodded. "Holmsby is a fine young gentleman. I have heard nothing but praise for him."

Vanessa smiled. "He seems so to me. But I do believe the two young gentlemen are running neck and neck in Millie's esteem."

"Neck and neck?" Stephen chuckled. "It is a race, then?"

"Most surely, and Millie is the prize. She asked for my opinion of the two gentlemen, and I have given it. But I must warn you she was not pleased with my answer."

"You said you preferred Holmsby?"

"Yes, I did, but I dared not share the full extent of my worries about Mr. Woodhouse with her."

Stephen's eyebrows shot up in surprise. "Why not?"

"Millie is what Papa would call the champion of the unfortunate. She is too kindhearted to agree with a negative assessment of Mr. Woodhouse's character."

"Even if she suspects we are correct and Woodhouse leaves much to be desired as a suitor for her?"

Vanessa nodded. "If we roundly criticize Mr. Woodhouse, Millie will defend him, and that could result in the very action we fear. We must have proof before we accuse Woodhouse of wrongdoing, Stephen—irrefutable proof Millie cannot fail to recognize."

"You are quite right." Stephen slipped his arm round her shoulders. "I am relieved to discuss this with you. Perhaps I am overly protective of Millie, but I cannot help fearing Woodhouse is up to no good where she is concerned."

Vanessa smiled as she settled against his side. If she could stay like this forever, she would be happy. But she must not be lulled into complacency by Stephen's friendly embrace. Though she desired it above all things, they were discussing a very serious problem. "I have no doubt you have queried your acquaintances regarding Mr. Woodhouse. What have you learned of him?"

"Not enough of value, certainly." Stephen pulled her a bit closer and Vanessa had all she could do to keep her thoughts on the problem at hand. "But there are rumors Woodhouse has been asking about Millie's marriage settlement."

Vanessa winced. "Oh, dear! You believe he is serious, then, in his pursuit of Millie?"

"I do. We must gather more information about him, Vanessa. I have heard nothing to disparage his character, but he is not well liked. Perhaps we are calling the kettle black when it is merely tarnished, but we must make certain for Millie's sake."

"Yes. Will you attempt to learn more about Mr. Woodhouse?"

"Of course. I shall resume my inquiry the moment I return to town."

"You are leaving?" Vanessa did not wish to be left alone with this problem, away from Stephen's comforting presence.

"I must go away for a fortnight. I have pressing business to complete, and it cannot wait upon my convenience. I should like to stay and see this matter settled, but I cannot."

"I shall keep a sharp eye while you are away, Stephen. I shall make certain Millie will not be led astray by Mr. Woodhouse."

"You look quite fierce—very like a mother cat defending her kitten."

Vanessa smiled. "Precisely. While Millie is in my charge, she shall not come to any harm. I shall endeavor to learn more about Mr. Woodhouse and his circumstances."

"You must take all caution." The grim look did not leave Stephen's eyes. "If Woodhouse is the cad I believe him to be, he will not wish to be exposed."

"I shall take your warning to heart and govern myself accordingly. You must not worry on my account."

"But I will worry." Stephen's arm tightened around her and he pulled her even closer. "You are very dear to me."

Vanessa took a shivering breath. Dared she voice what was in her heart? He appeared to be waiting for her answer, and Vanessa found she could not disappoint him. "I share your sentiments, Stephen. You are also very dear to me."

"I have waited long years to hear those words." Stephen smiled, his first genuine smile, and gathered her in a close embrace. "I must be honest with you, my dear, for my heart is heavy with this burden."

Vanessa stared up at him in surprise, trembling slightly at the pleasure of his embrace. Her lips parted in wonder, and before she could think to pull back, he lowered his lips to hers and kissed her passionately.

Her mind was spinning out of control. Vanessa felt as if the very heavens had opened as she returned his kiss in full measure. She had dreamed of this moment for so long.

"I love you, Vanessa." Stephen's voice was soft. "And I know you love me, too."

Vanessa sighed as his lips lowered to hers again and she felt the strength of his love for her. She did not think, *could* not think, as he drank of her lips and their bodies melded together in a burst of passion greater than anything she had ever imagined. Did this desire to be one with him in mind and body make up the substance of love? It must, for her only wish was to be with Stephen like this for eternity.

She was not certain how long their kiss lasted. There was only Stephen and their love for each other, timeless and endless. But a chill invaded her happiness as one small corner of her mind remembered Stephen was married. She had no right to kiss him like this. There was his wife to consider.

"Stephen!" Vanessa pulled out of his embrace, tears streaming down her face. "You cannot! We cannot! You must not forget your wife!"

He stared down at her and then laughed bitterly. "How could I forget her? I curse the day I married her. She has ruined my life."

"But . . . but you must have loved her." Vanessa's voice trembled.

"Never!" Stephen spat out the comment. "She duped me from the start. I should have known better. Now only death will release her unholy hold on me."

Vanessa stared up at him in shock. The gentleman she had loved for so long wished his wife were dead. "Please do not say words you will later regret. It is wrong for you to speak ill of your wife in her father's home."

"You are quite right." Stephen nodded, but his voice was hard. "I hold Charles in great esteem and I should not like him to know what a worthless chit his daughter has turned out to be. He will not learn the truth from me, not when he is so ill and helpless."

Vanessa could say nothing. Her emotions were in a hopeless muddle, but tears fell from her eyes and she shuddered at the force of his hatred.

"I have nothing but disgust for my wife, Vanessa, and Phoebe has nothing but disgust for me. It was an ill-fated match bound to end in tragedy. But you have taught me what love is. I love you with all my heart. It is not right Phoebe should keep us apart. Love me, Vanessa, and be with me always. I cannot marry you, but you will be my true wife, I swear it. We must not let Phoebe stand in the way of our happiness."

He reached out to pull her back into his arms, but Vanessa struggled against him. "No! What you suggest is a . . . a travesty! Perhaps you can forget your marriage vows, but I cannot!"

"Please, my darling, let me explain." Stephen succeeded in pulling her into his arms. "My marriage is nothing but a sham. Phoebe did not want me as a wife wants her husband. We are married in name only."

Vanessa shivered as she stared up into his desperate eyes. She had misjudged him dreadfully. His wife was ill and not able to be a true wife to him, and now he wanted her to replace Phoebe in his bed.

"You are despicable!" Vanessa gave vent to the full measure of her disappointment and her wrath. "How dare you try to seduce me in your papa-in-law's home? You are nothing but an unfaithful cad!"

Vanessa did not wait to see his reaction to her words. It would make no difference. She tore herself from his arms and fled down the garden path. Her skirts caught against the thorns of the roses, but she did not stop to free them. She allowed the fabric to rip and continued her headlong flight.

There was no one on the staircase and Vanessa gave silent thanks that no one would witness the sobs threatening to tear from her throat and the tears cascading down her cheeks. She rushed up the steps, ran swiftly down the corridor, and did not halt until she had reached her door. Once inside, with the door locked securely behind her, Vanessa sank down on the edge of her bed.

The gentleman she loved with all of her being had shown his true self this day, and he had turned out to be a despicable cad, willing to forsake his wedding vows by attempting to seduce her in his wife's childhood home. How could she have failed to see the true reason he had brought her to London, away from her papa and all her friends? He had planned to seduce her all along, but he had misjudged her. She was no hen-witted country girl who would tumble into his bed without knowing right from wrong.

Oh, but she *had* loved him. He had been right about that. Vanessa blushed to think of how she had responded to his kisses, how her body had trembled and come close to betraying her when he had held her in his arms. She had desired to throw caution to the winds, to agree to everything he had suggested, but she hadn't and she was glad. She had done the honorable thing. No one could expect more of her.

But the loss of all her secret hopes and dreams was more than Vanessa could bear. In the privacy of her bedchamber, with no one to witness her grief, she gave way to the desolate sobs that accompanied her broken heart.

Fourteen

Vanessa frowned as she gazed at her reflection in the mirror. Her eyes were still slightly swollen from crying, but she had told Colette a bit of dust had blown into her face while she was walking in the garden, and she had dispatched the abigail to the kitchens for a cucumber. Thinly sliced, it tightened the skin around the eyes and reduced the effects of prolonged tears. She had also vowed Millie should never learn of her brother's duplicity.

After her tears were spent, Vanessa thought long and hard about her encounter with Stephen in the gardens. She must accept part of the blame for his indecent proposal. She had encouraged his attentions. Vanessa suspected when she returned Stephen's kiss, she had led him to believe she would welcome his further advances.

Never one to shirk her responsibilities, Vanessa had shouldered her part of the blame for the unfortunate fiasco. That did not mean she had forgiven Stephen. Instead, she resolved from this day forward, their relationship would be circumspect. When the Season was concluded and it was time to remove to Bridgeford Hall once again, she would resign and take herself out of harm's way.

"I do believe your cucumber has done its work well." Colette leaned closer to examine Vanessa's eyes. "They are not as swollen as they were only moments ago. Does it also serve for one who cries?"

Vanessa glanced sharply at her abigail, but she could not judge whether Colette had guessed the true source of her swollen eyes. "I am certain it would. Cucumber eases swollen eyes, regardless of the reason."

"I must remember this if I choose to accept a position with a mistress who turns into a watering pot at the slightest provocation." Colette dropped her eyes, but not before Vanessa saw the gleam of sympathy in their brown depths.

"I did not cry." It was difficult to tell an untruth to the abigail who had become her friend. "As I mentioned earlier, a cloud of dust blew into my eyes."

Colette nodded. "Dust. Yes, indeed. I did not doubt it for a moment, Miss Vanessa. But there is no shame in indulging in tears when one's heart is aching. It is a most natural and therapeutic action to take."

"Has Lord Bridgeford taken his leave?" Vanessa decided the wisest course would be to change the subject.

"Yes, his coach departed two hours ago. You had best hurry if you are at all sharp set. Lady Treverton has asked you and Millie to join her for a light repast before you attend Lady Whittaker's musicale."

"I do wish I were not required to go, but I suppose there is no help for it."

"No, indeed." A smile turned up the corners of Colette's lips. "M'lady may require your support on this night."

"My support? Whatever for?"

"I have been in Lady Treverton's employ for the past six years and I have noticed she frequently suffers an attack of the megrims before the conclusion of one of Lady Whittaker's musicales."

Vanessa frowned slightly. "That is unfortunate. Perhaps I should bring a remedy with me, in the event Aunt Lolly requires my assistance."

"No, indeed not!" Colette leaned closer, her eyes twinkling with amusement. "I have heard Lady Whittaker's musicales are quite tedious. I suspect m'lady's malady is an excuse of convenience. It allows her to depart without insult to her hostess. Your remedy might defeat her true purpose."

Vanessa grinned. "Thank you for telling me, Colette. If Aunt Lolly complains of a malady, I shall insist she return home immediately, and I shall accompany her to provide my assistance."

"That is the very thing I had in mind. But you must not leave Miss Millie behind, for she mentioned Mr. Woodhouse will also attend the musicale."

Vanessa's eyebrows shot up. Colette had noticed all was not as it seemed with Mr. Woodhouse. "You are a wealth of information. Now that we have broached the subject of Mr. Woodhouse, I would regard it as a favor if you would give me your opinion of him."

"I dare not." Colette shook her head, apparently wishing she had not spoken so freely. "It is not for me to pass judgment on my betters."

Vanessa reached out for Colette's hand. "Do not grow fainthearted now. I know you have an opinion, and I should like to hear it. You may rest assured I will not repeat it. I merely wish to compare your assessment of Mr. Woodhouse to the one I have formed."

"You are certain, Miss Vanessa?"

"I am," Vanessa assured her. "Please tell me."

Colette glanced at the door to make certain it was shut, and then moved a bit closer. "I doubt Mr. Woodhouse *is* a gentleman. I have encountered many of his type in the past. Miss Millie is thoroughly taken in by him, and this worries me greatly. She regards every pretty word that leaves his lips as truth. You are wise to take precautions, and I hope I have not spoken out of turn."

"Thank you, Colette." Vanessa smiled. "You have bolstered my opinion of Mr. Woodhouse. I know Millie often speaks to you in confidence, and I beg you to seek me out immediately if you believe he presents a threat to her."

Colette nodded. "Miss Millie is naïf, and I fear she is fair game for his sweet words and empty promises. I shall come to you with all haste if I learn of any danger to her."

Vanessa rose from her chair, noting her eyes had resumed their natural state. She gave Colette a parting smile and left the room, much more at ease about the situation with Millie and Mr. Woodhouse. Vanessa had no doubt the abigail would guard Millie as carefully as Vanessa planned to. With two pairs of watchful eyes, they should succeed in averting any disaster.

"I still do not understand why we had to leave so early." Millie sighed as she climbed the stairs to her chamber. "Aunt Lolly did not seem to be that ill."

Vanessa kept her expression perfectly composed. Lady Whittaker's musicale had been dreadful, and she could not blame Aunt Lolly for serving up a convenient excuse to return home. "Maladies of this nature may come upon one very suddenly, Millie."

"But she appears perfectly fit now." Millie frowned petulantly. "And I do not understand why I was forced to accompany you. Wood . . . Mr. Woodhouse quite properly offered to escort me home once the evening was concluded."

"We could not leave you there, dearest, without a suitable chaperone."

"But I *had* a chaperone. I had two of them. Miss Agatha Ramsey and her sister, Miss Ivy, agreed to ride with us in Mr. Woodhouse's carriage while he carried me home."

"Two unmarried misses are not suitable chaperones for a debutante, Millie." Vanessa sighed. She had known Millie would be put out, but her patience was beginning to wear thin. "The Ramsey sisters have been the subject of several alarming *on-dits*."

Millie's lower lip extended slightly in a pout. "Surely you do not believe all the gossip tabbies of the *ton* bandy about. I am certain Agatha and Ivy have been maligned for no good reason."

Vanessa knew better than to argue with Millie when she was in such high dudgeon. "That may very well be true. But this is your debutante Season, and you must take heed of the rumors, whether or not they are true. I see no harm in befriending Miss Ramsey and her sister when you encounter them at parties and such, but riding alone in the carriage with them, with Mr. Woodhouse in attendance, may hinder your chances of making an excellent match."

"I may have made my perfect match." Millie's eyes sparkled and her demeanor changed completely. The petulant child was transformed into a giddy young lady. "Do come in for a comfy coze, Vanessa, and I shall tell you all. And let us ring for a tray, as we have missed Lady Whittaker's refreshments."

Vanessa followed Millie into the sitting room they shared. "I should not be anxious about the refreshments we have forfeited, Millie. I have heard Lady Whittaker is regrettably cheeseparing and her table leaves much to be desired."

Millie giggled, her good humor completely restored. "Then perhaps it is as well we took our leave. Let us have cups of chocolate and cakes, and while we are waiting for our tray to arrive, let us put on our night rails and wrappers. I have missed the talks we were used to have when we were in the country."

Vanessa rang for the tray and then went off to her bedchamber to remove her gown and prepare for bed. She was not inclined to a comfy coze about matches and suitors, but perhaps some good might come of it. Millie wished to confide in her, and it was possible she would listen to Vanessa's opinion about Mr. Woodhouse.

It did not take long for Vanessa to hang her gown in the clothespress and put on her night rail and wrapper. Once she was ready, she padded across the rug on her slippered feet and entered the sitting room. The tray had been delivered in their absence, but Vanessa did not avail herself of its contents. Instead, she took a seat on the sofa, tucked her feet up under her warm wrapper and sighed as she thought of what might have occurred if Mr. Woodhouse had succeeded in his attempt to escort Millie home.

What she had told Millie about the Ramsey sisters had been the truth. According to Aunt Lolly, Miss Ivy narrowly escaped being compromised during her debutante Season by a young gentleman well known as a rakehell. Only the intervention of her brother had saved her from being carried off to Gretna by the object of her affections.

The older sister, Miss Agatha Ramsey, had committed several serious breaches of etiquette during Seasons past, not the least of which was becoming regrettably foxed at Lord and Lady Stanhope's wedding feast and tumbling into the ornamental pool in the garden.

Millie appeared in the doorway, wearing a lovely pink wrapper. "I am ready, Vanessa. Will you pour?"

"Of course." Vanessa poured the chocolate and patted the couch beside her. "Come and join me."

Millie lifted her skirts and raced across the floor, plopping down on the couch next to Vanessa and tucking up her feet. That made Vanessa smile. She was childlike in so many ways, and naive in the giving of her affections. Millie trusted others implicitly, never doubting they were not all she believed them to be. It was little wonder the sinfully handsome Mr. Woodhouse had succeeded in gaining her good auspices.

"I do believe Mr. Woodhouse intends to declare for me at the Valentine's Day Ball." Millie's smile was radiant.

"We have not discussed the matter, of course, but he has led me to believe he is on the verge of asking Stephen for my hand."

"Are you certain?" Vanessa took care no chink appeared in her composure.

"Yes—at least, I think I am. He has spoken to me of his circumstances and his family. That means he is serious in his pursuit of me, does it not?"

"He would certainly appear to be. But there is also the possibility Mr. Woodhouse is, by nature, outspoken. Do you know if he has been as candid with any other young ladies of his acquaintance?"

"I am certain he has not." Millie sipped her chocolate and reached out to take a poppy-seed cake. "It is just as I told you. Wood . . . Mr. Woodhouse has told me everything. He has even spoken to me of the improvements he wishes to make on his estate."

"Mr. Woodhouse has an estate? I thought he was the third son of a baron."

"He is." Millie smiled. "He is forever telling me I am too far above him socially. Of course, I refuse to listen. You have taught me that, Vanessa. I know a person's status has very little to do with his character and his true worth."

Millie was saying the correct and responsible things, but she still viewed Mr. Woodhouse through a glass colored by her affections. Vanessa was certain these affections were misplaced, but she could not prove that to Millie. "I am confused, Millie. I assumed Mr. Woodhouse did not *have* an estate."

"He does not, but he will soon buy one. He receives an allowance from his father, and he has been saving every penny he can for his estate. He does not drink or gamble or go to clubs where he might be tempted to do so. He is living quite frugally, and he has no expenses to speak of."

Vanessa could not help smiling. "There is his tailor."

"Of course. I forgot about that. But Mr. Woodhouse receives a substantial discount by referring others to his tailor. It is a business arrangement, you see, and his clothing does not cost much."

"I see." Vanessa kept the smile on her face, even though she suspected Mr. Woodhouse was heavily in debt to his tailor. "Has he given a thought to where he will buy his estate?"

"He is not certain, but I am convinced it will be far away from his father's estate in the Lake District. He prefers a milder climate."

Vanessa nodded, keeping her thoughts to herself. She had learned the whereabouts of Baron Woodhouse's estate, and that might be of value. "Tell me, Millie, if Mr. Woodhouse does declare for you, as you anticipate, what are your desires in the matter?"

"Why, I should accept him, of course." Millie giggled charmingly. "How could I do otherwise?"

"Are you certain, then, you wish to marry Mr. Woodhouse?"

"Oh, yes, Vanessa! He is my perfect match, the most charming and fashionable gentleman I have ever met. Indeed, I cannot conceive of marrying another."

"Not even Lord Holmsby?" Vanessa held her breath as she waited for Millie's answer.

"Lord Holmsby?" A soft look came into Millie's eyes. "He is uncommonly nice, and I do like him very much. I regard him as a dear friend, the dearest gentleman friend I have ever had."

"But you would not consider accepting Lord Holmsby's declaration, should he tender it?"

"If I had not met Wood . . . Mr. Woodhouse, I should have been tempted to marry Lord Holmsby. He would make such an excellent husband."

"But now that you have met Mr. Woodhouse, you have

decided you do not love Lord Holmsby?" Again, Vanessa held her breath.

"I *do* love him! Lord Holmsby is all that is good, but he does not rouse my passions to the extent Mr. Woodhouse does. Perhaps he is just a bit too . . . too . . . I am not certain of the word."

"Too responsible?"

"Yes, precisely. Lord Holmsby is extremely loyal and faithful, the very gentleman I would call upon if I found myself in a horrible bumblebroth. He would extricate me immediately and never once call me to task on my mistake. I would also seek him out if I needed an important task accomplished in a careful manner and with great dispatch. He is reliable, and I am convinced he has my best interests at heart."

"Do you regard Lord Holmsby as handsome?"

"Indeed, I do. He is well-favored in both face and disposition."

"And do you think Lord Holmsby would be a good father?"

A smile lit up Millie's face. "He would be perfection. I cannot imagine him flying off over a childish prank or a bit of mischief. He is admirably even-tempered, and he possesses a wonderful sense of humor."

"And how do you regard Mr. Woodhouse in these areas?"

"He would also be fine." Millie's smile faded a bit. "He does have a bit of a temper, but I am convinced he would keep it in check when dealing with his children. And though he does not possess the fine sense of humor Lord Holmsby enjoys, that is quite understandable. He has many more worries to plague him."

"He does?" Vanessa raised her eyebrows, encouraging Millie to tell her more.

"Lord Holmsby's future is assured. He has inherited his father's title and need have no anxiety about money or property. Mr. Woodhouse must make his own way in the world, and that is a constant worry to him."

Vanessa filed the information away and nodded. "And even though Lord Holmsby is perfection in every way, you would rather marry Mr. Woodhouse?"

"Of course! I have tumbled into love with Mr. Woodhouse, Vanessa, and such exciting and passionate love cannot be denied. I simply must marry him!"

After a few more minutes, Millie claimed she was exhausted and must seek her bed. Vanessa stacked their cups on the tea tray and sighed as she walked to her own bedchamber.

Millie recognized Lord Holmsby's good qualities, and she had admitted she loved him. But she had *tumbled into love* with Mr. Woodhouse.

Vanessa wished there were some way to tell Millie such exciting and passionate love was transitory, without a solid base beneath it. Stephen had awakened such exciting and passionate love in her, but Vanessa's love crumbled the moment Stephen had made the indecent proposal that she forget the existence of his wife and become his mistress.

Rather than dwell on her own painful disappointment, Vanessa climbed into bed and stared up at the ceiling, thinking of Millie's welfare. The coze she had enjoyed with Millie had not convinced Vanessa. There was something havey-cavey about Mr. Woodhouse, and she would uncover it.

A thought crossed Vanessa's mind just as she was drifting to sleep. She sat upright in bed, a relieved smile upon her face. Aunt Lolly had mentioned Charles possessed a minor estate in the Lake Country. She had also stated they had not traveled there for some years, but Charles had spent much time there before they were wed.

Vanessa felt hopeful. Though the area was large and it would be a remarkable coincidence, she was resolved to ask Charles at the first opportunity whether he'd had occasion to meet Baron Woodhouse and his sons.

There was little time to waste. If Millie's predictions proved accurate, Mr. Woodhouse would declare himself at the Valentine's Day Ball in less than two weeks' time. The more information she could garner about Mr. Woodhouse and his family before then, the better it would bode for Millie's future happiness.

Fifteen

Vanessa was up long before any other member of the household the following morning, but she could eat little for breakfast. She had slept poorly, waking at the slightest noise to mull over what seemed to be insurmountable obstacles.

Her emotions were in a terrible muddle. As Vanessa sat in solitude in the breakfast room, she attempted to clarify them. Though she despised Stephen for his callous disregard of his marriage vows, it did not diminish the physical attraction she still harbored for him. He was not the gentleman she thought she loved, but she loved him all the same, and she was certain she must not allow herself to be tempted by his embrace again.

Vanessa smiled bitterly. Her love for Stephen could be the sort of love Millie entertained for Mr. Woodhouse. How could they have come to this unhappy turn? They were, both of them, in love with scoundrels, and a woman who loved a scoundrel could never respect herself. As difficult as it was, they must harden their hearts against these unsuitable emotions.

But was Mr. Woodhouse a scoundrel? Vanessa was still not certain. She must settle the matter without a shadow of a doubt before she attempted to warn Millie away from him. To do otherwise would be grossly unfair. She was required to give Mr. Woodhouse the benefit of the doubt until the evidence proved otherwise.

Vanessa glanced at the standing clock in the corner of the breakfast room and pushed back her chair with resolve. Charles also rose early and should be awake and dressed by this hour. She would ask his help in solving the riddle of Mr. Woodhouse.

The corridors were deserted except for a footman and two maids. Vanessa slowed her steps and nodded politely as she passed them. It would not do to have it bandied about in the servants' quarters that she had rushed headlong down the halls. Aunt Lolly would hear of it, and it would prompt her to ask questions better left unanswered.

The door to Charles's quarters stood open, and two maids were busy dusting the furniture and emptying the grate. The servants were not allowed to straighten the chambers while Charles was there, and their presence told Vanessa he had already left. She hurried to the study, where she found Charles sitting behind his desk.

"Vanessa." Charles smiled as she appeared in his doorway. "You are up early this morn."

"I simply could not wait any longer to see you. I have a matter of grave importance to put to you."

"Come in and have tea with me." Charles gestured toward the tea tray on the top of his desk. "I will ring for another cup."

"Thank you, but I have had my fill of tea this morning. I should prefer to get the crux of the matter, if you do not mind."

"Certainly." Charles nodded as she took a chair. "What is it, Vanessa? You appear overset."

"It is Millie. She confided to me she expects to receive a declaration at the Valentine's Day Ball."

"I see. And will this declaration come from Lord Holmsby or from Mr. Woodhouse?"

Vanessa eyebrows shot up in surprise. "Then you have been informed Millie has suitors?"

"Indeed, I have. Lolly has told me all. Which young

gentleman has gathered sufficient courage to tender an offer for her hand?"

"It is Mr. Woodhouse, I fear. Stephen has charged me with the duty of making certain he is a suitable match for Millie."

"I see." Charles leaned back in his chair, taking on a solemn expression. "And you are not convinced Woodhouse is suitable?"

"Precisely. I have learned nothing that disabuses the notion, but before Stephen left, he mentioned he had heard a rumor at his club that Mr. Woodhouse has been inquiring about Millie's marriage settlement."

"And this interest in Millie's assets has caused you to doubt Mr. Woodhouse's sincerity?"

"Yes. I have also received other impressions from the gentleman himself that cause me to doubt him."

"You must tell me of these impressions." Charles smiled at her. "I assure you our converse shall be confidential."

"I never doubted that. As I told you, these are merely impressions, and I could very well be in error."

"Go on."

"He is as polished as the rocks at the bottom of a fast-moving stream. His manners are perfection, his compliments to Millie slide easily from his tongue, and I have never viewed him in less than perfect composure. He has no faults—he does not drink, gamble, or have a roving eye. And though Millie has said he has a bit of a quick temper, it is under tight rein. I have watched him carefully. Mr. Woodhouse's comportment is without blemish."

"You believe he is too good to be true?"

"Yes." Vanessa sighed. "I suspect Mr. Woodhouse is hiding his true nature. Before Stephen left, I promised I would guard Millie carefully in his absence. I did not think things would come to a head this soon, but Millie has confided Mr. Woodhouse is about to offer for her."

"Yes. His character is of paramount importance," Charles said. "I shall be happy to help you, Vanessa, but you must tell me precisely how I can do so."

"Aunt Lolly mentioned that you own a small estate in the Lake District, and that is where Baron Woodhouse resides. Have you heard mention of the family?"

"I shall not be of much assistance on that score. I have not traveled to the Lake District for many years, and I do not believe I have met any family of that name. Unless . . ."

Charles stopped speaking and Vanessa leaned forward. "What is it?"

"I seem to remember my agent mentioning the name some six years past. As I recall, the family consisted of a father and three motherless sons."

"That could very well be Baron Woodhouse," Vanessa said. "I do know Mr. Woodhouse is the youngest of three sons."

Charles frowned thoughtfully. "I do not recall any more than the gist of it. It was something havey-cavey with one of the sons, but I cannot remember which one. What is this Woodhouse's age?"

"He is just turned twenty-two. Millie mentioned he celebrated his birthday no more than a month ago."

"Then he would have been sixteen at the time. If Woodhouse was the boy my agent mentioned, it could have been nothing but a prank."

"But you think it could have been more serious?"

"I do remember something, but I will not speak of it until I am certain." Charles pulled out a drawer and retrieved a piece of vellum. "I shall write to my agent immediately to ask him to refresh my memory and learn what he can of the family."

Vanessa smiled for the first time that morning. "Thank you. That is an excellent suggestion, and it will prove most helpful. And you will mention you require an immediate reply?"

"I shall light a fire under him—you may be certain of that. My agent is highly reliable, and he will not fail to reply by return post. We shall soon know if Woodhouse is a proper suitor for Millie."

"I do wish I could do more."

"Perhaps you can." Charles looked up from his letter with a thoughtful expression. "Millie has a second suitor, does she not?"

"Lord Holmsby. But how could he help?"

"You believe Holmsby is sincere in his affections toward Millie?"

"Yes, I am certain he is. From what I have observed, Lord Holmsby appears to be smelling of April and May."

Charles chuckled. "That is excellent. You must enlist his aid in uncovering Woodhouse's true character. After all, he is a rival suitor. He has much to gain if Woodhouse proves unsuitable."

Vanessa's eyes widened and she began to laugh. "You are devilishly clever. Who better to investigate a gentleman's character than his rival for Millie's affections?"

The butler caught Vanessa just as she was about to seek out Millie. "A letter arrived for you in the post, Miss Vanessa. I sent it up to your chamber with Colette."

"Thank you, Mr. Hodges." Vanessa smiled at the friendly butler and reversed her direction. No doubt it was a letter from her father, telling her all the news of Bridgeford Village. Though London was exciting and she had enjoyed most of the entertainments, Vanessa longed for her home. Of course, there *was* intrigue in Bridgeford Village, but on a much smaller scale and more easily dealt with.

When Vanessa reached her bedchamber, Colette was

gone, but the letter sat on the dressing table. Vanessa gasped as she spied it. It was from her secret admirer.

Vanessa smiled as she sat down on the edge of her bed to open it. Her secret admirer was resourceful. Somehow he had learned she was in London and had gained her direction.

Her fingers trembled as she broke the seal and unfolded the heavy cream-colored vellum. After her disappointment with Stephen and her worries regarding Millie, a letter from her secret admirer was a most welcome diversion.

My dearest Vanessa, the letter began. Vanessa smiled. Though Stephen had turned out to be a far different gentleman than she had believed him to be, her secret admirer was constant in his affections.

> *I am here in London, and my desire to see you is nearly overwhelming. But I shall wait until Valentine's Day to look once more upon your lovely countenance.*

Vanessa smiled. She did not look lovely today. There were dark circles under her eyes from lack of sleep, and her normally sunny disposition had all but disappeared.

> *I shall attend Lord and Lady Treverton's Valentine's Day Ball and shall look forward with the greatest pleasure to meeting you there. I have much to tell you, and it is past time to confess what is in my heart. I dream of you every night, my darling, and long to hold you in my arms. Certain unfortunate circumstances have made this impossible, but I am convinced the time is near when I shall be free to offer my love and urge you to become my wife.*

A sigh escaped Vanessa's lips and the ashes of her heart warmed. Perhaps her secret admirer was an admirable gentleman, a gentleman with whom she could have children and enjoy a contented family life. She could not love him, but she could grow fond of him, and many said fondness was all that was required in a marriage. Vanessa knew in her heart she would never love another gentleman with the burning desire she had felt for Stephen, but perhaps that was best. Such consuming love was an agony if the recipient did not return it in full measure.

I beg you to save me two waltzes, my dearest Vanessa. I ask you for the first and the last. It is my fondest hope our second waltz together shall be the beginning of a life of love.

Vanessa smiled a bit sadly, folding the letter and holding it close to her. Would her secret admirer be deeply disappointed when he found she could not love him the way he claimed to love her? Or would he forgive her unsuitable love for Stephen and accept her as she was? She would have to tell him if he were truly serious in his intentions. It would not be fair of her to marry this gentleman without divulging all of what was in her heart.

Could she marry her secret admirer when her heart still belonged to Stephen? Vanessa sighed, a worried frown furrowing her brow. She was not certain what she should do, and there was little time to dwell upon it. She would have to wait and see whether or not her secret admirer appeared at the Valentine's Day Ball.

Vanessa was about to hide the letter under the stack of handkerchiefs in her drawer when she remembered what her secret admirer had asked. He wished to dance the first and the last waltzes with her, and she had already promised them to Stephen. But after what had transpired between them in the gardens, Vanessa doubted Stephen would attempt to claim those waltzes. Instead, she would waltz with her secret admirer and pray he was not such a scoundrel as Stephen had turned out to be.

How would she know which gentleman her secret admirer was? Vanessa smiled at the thought of a crowd of gallants lined up before her, each requesting a waltz. She need have no worries on that score. But she would like to know her secret admirer's name in advance of his request to dance with her. How could she discover his identity?

Vanessa opened the letter once again, and reread the first few lines. A gentleman did not attend a ball unless he had received an invitation. All she need do was peruse the guest list to discover who her secret admirer might be.

"Gracious, Vanessa! You are completely out of breath." Aunt Lolly's eyes widened in surprise as Vanessa rushed into her private sitting room. "Is there something amiss?"

"No, Aunt Lolly. I merely wished to see the guest list for our Valentine's Day Ball."

"Of course." Aunt Lolly gestured toward the escritoire beneath the tall mullioned windows overlooking the gardens. "It is there, under the ink stand."

Vanessa forced herself to walk slowly to retrieve the list. "I am searching for a particular name."

"And which name would that be?"

Vanessa's mind spun with the effort of devising a plausible reason. She had not thought to prepare an excuse, and she did not want to tell Aunt Lolly of her secret admirer. "Papa has written that a gentleman of his acquaintance has received an invitation to our ball. He asked that I extend his greetings, but neglected to mention the gentleman's name."

"It is a puzzle, then." Aunt Lolly looked delighted. "I do adore puzzles. Perhaps I may be of some assistance to you, Vanessa, as I am certain I know everyone whose name is on our guest list. What do you know of this gentleman?"

"Merely that he is unmarried and has visited the area in which I live."

Aunt Lolly laughed. "That does not narrow the field overmuch, but I suppose it is a start. Read the names, dear, and I shall tell you what I know of them."

More than an hour went by as Vanessa read the names and Aunt Lolly described the individuals. When they had come to the last name on the list, they were no closer to solving the puzzle than when they began.

"There is no one else?" Vanessa frowned as she returned the list to its original place.

"Why, yes. There will be several dozen other guests."

"Who will they be?"

"I am not certain. I have issued several inclusive invitations."

"What is that, Aunt Lolly?" Vanessa had never heard of inclusive invitations.

"Families who live in town year-round often entertain visitors from the country. It is most convenient for cousins and other acquaintances who have no other place to stay and wish to avail themselves of the pleasures of the Season."

"I see." Vanessa nodded quickly. "And an inclusive invitation allows these families to bring their guests to the ball?"

"Certainly, dear. It would be bad *ton* not to include them in such a large affair."

"Which families have received such invitations?" Vanessa leaned forward eagerly. Perhaps her secret admirer did not reside in town and was merely visiting.

"Lord and Lady Ainsbrook frequently entertain visitors, and I have sent an inclusive invitation to them. And then there is Lady Martingale. I do believe her brother is here, along with his wife and one of their married daughters."

This line of questioning was useless. "I shall have to wait for this gentleman to approach me, Aunt Lolly. Perhaps I shall recognize him, and then all will be well."

The remainder of the day passed slowly for Vanessa. She took her place in the drawing room at the appointed hour, joining Aunt Lolly and Millie in receiving their visitors.

Millie truly seemed smitten with Mr. Woodhouse. Vanessa sighed as they sat on the couch, side by side, exchanging low comments. She had thought to speak to Lord Holmsby, but he did not call. He did send flowers, and Vanessa noted though Millie seemed properly impressed by his tribute, she quickly relegated the lovely bouquet to Mr. Hodges, to be arranged in a vase for the mantelpiece.

When their visitors had departed, Vanessa and Millie climbed the stairs to their chambers. Millie's eyes shone with excitement, and a small current of fear ran through Vanessa. "You look quite radiant."

"I am supremely happy—that is all. Mr. Woodhouse has told me of his success in rearranging the seating at Lady Bingham's dinner party this evening. You are to be on one side and I am to be on the other."

"How clever of him."

"Yes, indeed. He is nothing if not clever." Millie did not seem to notice Vanessa's lack of good humor, for she gave a radiant smile. "He has also requested I save the first dance for him, and the last."

Vanessa frowned at this information. "You must not dance more than two times with him of an evening, Millie."

"I am well aware of the proprieties, Vanessa. And I know I must follow them to the letter, though Woody and I regard them as silly."

Vanessa did not comment on Millie's use of Mr. Woodhouse's familiar name. She was simply too downhearted to chastise Millie. "Shall you take a rest now?"

"Indeed, I will." Millie smiled. "I must be well rested if I am to dance until the wee hours of the morning—and that is precisely what I plan to do."

Vanessa walked slowly down the corridor to her chamber. This had been a most unfruitful day. She could do nothing to speed the reply from Charles's agent; she must wait for it to come in the post. She had not succeeded in revealing the identity of her secret admirer, and she hadn't been able to request Lord Holmsby's aid. In light of Millie's newest revelation regarding the seating arrangements at Lady Bingham's dinner, she could not let down her guard. She would have to keep Millie under close observation not only during the dancing, but at Lady Bingham's table, as well.

She would attempt to speak to Mr. Holmsby this evening, but it would be difficult in the crush of guests. The proprieties must be observed, and she dared not be seen in close converse with him for more than a few moments. If only she could arrange to speak to him in strict privacy.

Vanessa could not call upon Lord Holmsby in person. An unmarried miss was forbidden to call upon a gentleman alone unless he was a relative. If she arrived at Lord Holmsby's town house with a suitable chaperone in tow, it would defeat the purpose of her visit.

She could send him a letter. Vanessa rushed to her writing table for paper and ink. She would not commit to paper her concerns for Millie, lest her letter fall into the wrong hands. Instead, she would ask Lord Holmsby to arrange a meeting with her at a suitable location where they could speak in relative privacy. She would also impress upon him the urgency of her petition and plead that their meeting take place this very afternoon. If Lord Holmsby was as resourceful as she believed him to be, he would comply with her request.

Sixteen

Vanessa stared down at Lord Holmsby's reply and gave a most unladylike whoop of delight. He was indeed resourceful. He would arrive within the hour to escort her to Gunther's for ices. His elderly aunt would accompany them to observe the proprieties, but Vanessa should not be concerned over their privacy, as Aunt Florence was regrettably afflicted with a severe hearing loss.

Rather than summoning Colette and suffering a barrage of questions about her destination and her companion, Vanessa quickly donned a suitable gown. Once she had brushed her hair, she turned to smile at her reflection in the mirror. Why had she not thought to cut her hair before? This new style was flattering and easily arranged without the assistance of a dresser. She gathered up her gloves, her reticule, and her pelisse. In no time at all, she was waiting for Lord Holmsby in the drawing room.

Lord Holmsby was as good as his word. He arrived only moments after Vanessa had entered the drawing room, and she quickly accompanied him to his waiting carriage. Once the introductions had been made, Lord Holmsby instructed his driver to spring the horses, and they arrived at Gunther's in short order.

"I do love Gunther's." Aunt Florence smiled as the ices arrived at their table. "Do not be concerned over me, dear John. I shall be quite content to enjoy my treat while you converse with your young lady."

"Thank you. I did recall this was your very favorite place."

"Face? There is something amiss with your face?"

"No, Aunt Florence." Lord Holmsby exchanged a speaking glance with Vanessa. "I said this is your FAVORITE PLACE."

"Indeed, it is. Get on with it, nephew. You must attend to your young lady. She is a contessa, you say?"

Vanessa smiled and leaned close to Aunt Florence's ear. "Vanessa. My name is VANESSA."

"How charming." Aunt Florence patted her hand. "Vanessa the contessa. It suits you perfectly. Now you must not bother any further with me. John has something he wishes to discuss with you."

"What is wrong, Miss Holland?" Lord Holmsby lowered his voice and leaned close so they could speak more easily. "You stated in your letter that the matter was urgent."

"It is indeed urgent. I fear Millie may be about to make a drastic error in judgment. But before I tell you the particulars, I must make certain you will treat this matter with the utmost discretion."

"You have my word."

"And may I have your assurance you hold Millie's best interests at heart?"

"Lady Thurston's happiness is of the greatest concern to me both now and in the future."

Vanessa smiled. Lord Holmsby had said precisely what she hoped. He had as much as admitted he intended to declare for Millie. "Millie expects Mr. Woodhouse to declare for her at the Valentine's Day Ball."

Lord Holmsby looked stunned at this news. "Woodhouse?"

"Yes, indeed. And her brother the earl and I are quite concerned about this turn of events."

Lord Holmsby's brows rose. "You do not approve of this match?"

"I do not, and the earl shares my concern. Perhaps it is regrettably unfair of me, but I doubt Mr. Woodhouse has Millie's best interests at heart. Unfortunately, I cannot find any proof."

"What are Lady Thurston's feelings on this matter?"

"I fear she has been thoroughly taken in by Mr. Woodhouse's charm and cannot see past his stylish appearance and lavish compliments. Millie is a complete innocent, you see, and I do not doubt Mr. Woodhouse has taken full advantage of that fact. She is not inclined to look past the outer trappings to see the real man inside."

"But you have done so, Miss Holland?"

"I have *attempted* to do so. Unfortunately, I have not succeeded in discrediting the man. Lord Holmsby . . ." Vanessa faltered, uncertain how to proceed. "May I call you John?"

"Of course."

"You must call me Vanessa. I know it is most unusual, but I find it difficult to converse on such a delicate subject while I am *my lording* you."

"Quite so!" Lord Holmsby chuckled. "Let us pretend to be as close as brother and sister, and speak what is in our hearts. You have guessed I plan to declare for Millie?"

"I had hoped as much. It is the reason I came to you with this problem. Neither Stephen nor I doubt your sincerity. But we do suspect there is something havey-cavey about Mr. Woodhouse."

"Perhaps I will be able to help you, Vanessa. Woodhouse has approached me on several occasions and invited me to join him of an evening."

"And you refused him?"

"I did. You see, I also suspect he is not all he appears to be and wish to avoid his company."

Vanessa smiled. "But now you will accept his offer?"

"Yes. If there are hidden aspects to his character, an

evening spent in his company may serve to ferret them out."

"Parrot?" Aunt Florence turned to him in surprise. "I see no parrot, John. Where is it?"

Vanessa leaned closer to the elderly lady. "Carat, Aunt Florence. Your nephew was remarking that the Prince Regent's new gem must be at least a CARAT."

"More, I should think." Aunt Florence nodded sagely. "Prinny would not have anything small. All one need do is gaze at the grand chandelier in his Crimson Drawing Room to know that."

Lord Holmsby grinned as Vanessa turned back to him. "You are quick on your feet. I was still attempting to rhyme with ferret."

"Thank you." Vanessa smiled. "What of your evening with Mr. Woodhouse? Would it be possible to arrange it soon?"

"I shall make the attempt this evening at Lady Bingham's dinner. No doubt Woodhouse shall take his leave shortly after your party has departed. I plan to approach him then."

"Do exercise all caution."

"Do not be anxious on my account. I have encountered his ilk before, and you must not forget I am forewarned."

"Your tea is not warmed?" Aunt Florence turned to her nephew. "Give me your cup, John, and I will pour you fresh."

John exchanged another speaking glance with Vanessa as he held out his cup and his aunt filled it. "Thank you, Aunt Florence. Would you care for another TRAY OF ICES?"

"How very nice of you, John. I do believe I would. The lemon was particularly tasty."

After John had ordered more ices, Vanessa posed a suggestion. "Perhaps your Aunt Florence might make use of an ear trumpet to hear more clearly."

"An ear trumpet?"

"Yes. It is simple, really. It amplifies sound through a cone that is held to the ear. My elderly cousin used one for several years before he passed on, and I am certain Papa still has it. I would be happy to write and ask him to send it, if your aunt would like to see it."

Lord Holmsby smiled. "Please do. Aunt Florence has told me she misses the converse she was used to enjoy in the drawing room. It could do much to enhance her life."

"Wife?" Aunt Florence turned to her nephew with alarm. "Good heavens, John! Did you just ask this lovely young lady to become your wife?"

Vanessa was exhausted by the time she returned home from Lady Bingham's dinner party. Keeping Millie out of harm's way was becoming quite difficult. Not only did she suspect Millie and Mr. Woodhouse had been holding hands beneath the dinner table, their comportment at the dance that followed had been on the very edge of scandal. If not for Lord Holmsby's sharp eye, Vanessa would have failed in the promise she had given Stephen to keep Millie safe from Mr. Woodhouse.

Soon after the dancing began, Millie and Mr. Woodhouse had escaped to a secluded spot on the balcony behind one of Lady Bingham's potted trees. John had spotted them leaving. Rather than waste precious minutes in alerting her, he had interrupted their tryst by seeking Millie out to ask her to dance. He'd told Vanessa Millie appeared disappointed to be interrupted, but she had done the proper thing and returned to the ballroom to dance with him.

Vanessa had taken Millie to task, but her charge had exhibited no remorse. She had failed to see what the fuss was about, claiming Woody had only wished to speak to her away from the crush and the noise. Millie had been sincere in her insistence nothing improper had occurred. Vanessa was convinced Millie had told the truth.

She'd cautioned Millie over the mere *appearance* of impropriety and extracted her promise she would not go off alone with Mr. Woodhouse again. Then Vanessa enjoyed a waltz with John. He, too, had been concerned over Millie's behavior and assured her with both of them alert, there would be no more unfortunate incidents on this particular night.

All the same, Vanessa had spent the remainder of the evening, which passed much too slowly to suit her, wondering whether Millie would have been compromised if not for John's timely intervention.

"Colette." Vanessa looked up in surprise as her abigail entered the chamber. "There is no need to attend me tonight. You should be abed."

Colette shook her head. "I have just come from Miss Millie's chamber and I fear she is most overset."

"What is it now?" Though Vanessa loved Millie dearly, supervising her was growing tedious in the extreme.

"I do not like to carry tales, but I must tell you Miss Millie has received a private *communiqué* from Mr. Woodhouse. It fell from her gown when I hung it in the clothespress, and I believe it is the source of her unhappiness."

Vanessa did not like to hear Millie was unhappy, but she must learn the content of this message from Mr. Woodhouse. "Did you happen to read it, Colette?"

"Yes." Colette hung her head. "I did not like to do so, but my concern for her future overrode any question of privacy. Have I done wrong?"

"No, you have done right. Tell me what Mr. Woodhouse has written."

"He wrote that he loved her, but you did not approve of him. He said he feared you would attempt to discredit him in her eyes. He accused the earl also, and said you

were in league with him to force Millie to marry a nobleman of more means than he possessed."

"Mr. Woodhouse suspects we are on to him."

Colette nodded. "There is more. He begged Millie not
to be swayed by anything you or the earl might say about
him and insisted every confidence he had shared with
Millie was the truth. And then he posed a question to her.
I am certain it is the reason she is so overset."

"What was the question?"

"He asked whether she would have the conviction to
believe in him and accept the truth in her heart, or
whether she was a child who would tumble to the lies you
and the earl would tell her."

Vanessa groaned softly. "He is devilishly clever, Colette,
and he has stacked the deck in his favor."

"How so?" Colette looked puzzled.

"Mr. Woodhouse is well aware Millie would like to cast
off her childish ways. It is natural when a young lady
reaches the brink of womanhood. Millie would like to
make her own decisions regarding her future."

"I felt the same when I was but fifteen. I believed I was
in love, but it was merely a childish infatuation. I am fortunate that my older brother stepped in and saved me
from making a terrible mistake."

"That is precisely Millie's ailment." Vanessa smiled at
Colette. "She is deep in the throes of a childish infatuation with the first gentleman who has shown an interest
in her. But you will remember I accused Mr. Woodhouse
of stacking the deck, Colette."

"You must explain it to me."

"Mr. Woodhouse has begged Millie to listen her imma-
ture heart, never admitting it shall lead her astray. At the
same time, he has suggested if Millie should choose to
listen to older and wiser heads, she will be acting as a
child who is still holding the apron strings of her brother
and companion."

Colette thought about this. "You are quite right. Millie does not wish to act as a child. She told me just yesterday she preferred I sleep in a room of my own, rather than the cot in her dressing room."

"Do you suppose . . . ?" Vanessa shivered, not able to utter the dire thought that crossed her mind.

Colette shrugged, understanding Vanessa's unspoken fear immediately. "I am not certain, Miss Vanessa. I cannot conceive she would attempt to run off with Mr. Woodhouse, but I thought to take all precautions. I told Miss Millie I would have to sleep in her dressing room for another few days until a chamber on the top floor became available."

"And she did not object?" Vanessa held her breath.

"No. She merely asked if the chamber would be ready by the night of m'lady's ball. I assured her it would, and she seemed quite content with my answer."

"She believes Mr. Woodhouse will declare for her that night. And if Stephen does not accept his offer, it seems Millie intends to take matters into her own hands."

"I assure you I shall sleep with one eye open in the event you are mistaken. Miss Millie will not run off before then, for I shall be vigilant."

"I have no doubt you will. And if the Fates are with us, it will not come to that. I simply must discredit Mr. Woodhouse."

Colette sighed. "It will take great persistence to do so. And even if you succeed in discrediting him, Miss Millie may not choose to believe you."

"I will force her to believe me." Vanessa gave a determined nod. "Millie cannot fail to accept the truth of Mr. Woodhouse's character if she confronts the evidence of his duplicity with her own eyes."

Seventeen

The strain was beginning to take its toll on Vanessa, and she gazed in the mirror with dismay. Colette had remarked that she had lost flesh, and Vanessa's reflection bore out the accuracy of that comment. Cook's best dishes, which Vanessa knew to be excellent, tasted like so much sawdust.

Vanessa's anxiety over Mr. Woodhouse had much to do with her loss of both appetite and sleep. But another worry had not ceased to plague her, a deep and compelling sadness she could do nothing to alleviate. Though the letter from her secret admirer had cheered her, Vanessa still found herself missing Stephen's company at the oddest times.

How could she miss him when she was so angry over what he had done? It was a conundrum. She despised his actions, and her eyes blazed with very real contempt when she remembered how he had attempted to give her a slip on the shoulder under his papa-in-law's roof. She knew full well she should hate Stephen, but she could not gather sufficient outrage to do so. Deep in her heart, Vanessa still loved him, and she suspected she always would.

Over the past few days, Vanessa had recalled Stephen's many kindnesses to her. She remembered their private moments and how he had never even hinted at any impropriety between them. She was almost willing to concede the incident in the gardens had been an aberration of his character, brought on by his overwhelming anxiety over Millie and Mr. Woodhouse. Perhaps in time she could accept his apology and forgive him, but she could not forget. Her response to Stephen's kisses should serve as a warning to her, a caution she should never allow herself to be placed in that position again.

"Vanessa, dear"—Aunt Lolly appeared in the doorway—"I have just come from Charles, and he would like the pleasure of your company in his study."

Vanessa rose from her dressing table. "Certainly, Aunt Lolly. Is something amiss?"

"No, dear. I believe it has to do with a letter he received moments ago by special messenger."

Vanessa managed a credible smile, though her heart was pounding with excitement. She moved sedately to the door, walked with Aunt Lolly to her chambers, and promised to join her in time to receive callers. But the moment Aunt Lolly's door had closed behind her, Vanessa picked up her skirts and fairly flew down the corridors to Charles's study, arriving flushed with exertion and regrettably out of breath.

"Vanessa. Come in, my dear, and take a chair." Charles looked up at her and smiled. "My agent has sent a reply."

Vanessa rushed forward and slid into the nearest chair. "What does it say?"

"I have not opened it." Charles held up the letter. "I was waiting for you."

"Please do not stand on ceremony. Let us see what it says."

Charles opened the letter and scanned the first few lines. "It appears you have the right of it, Vanessa. You were quite correct to be concerned over Mr. Woodhouse. It seems he left the Lake District to escape a scandal. My agent deems him a rake and a scoundrel, and I assure you he does not use those terms loosely."

"Please tell me the full particulars."

"Young Woodhouse is well known as a tosspot and a womanizer. Just four months ago, he fled his family estate in disgrace after compromising the young daughter of a local squire. The girl was but thirteen at the time, and she shall give birth to his bastard child before summer sets in."

"The poor girl!" Vanessa's eyes widened at this news. "And he refused to marry her?"

"He did. But that is not all, Vanessa." Charles looked up from the letter, his eyes filled with contempt for Mr. Woodhouse. "My agent also states he left massive gambling debts behind him. The young pup secured loans from his long-suffering father to redeem his vouchers, but instead he returned to the tables and gambled it all away."

Vanessa shook her head in dismay. This was indeed serious business. "Then his pockets are empty, with no prospect of filling them?"

"It is worse than that. Apparently young Woodhouse fell in with a gang of thieves. While the baron was away, they ransacked his family estate, and Baron Woodhouse is convinced his son had a part in it. The thieves made off with the family jewels. Only a member of the family would have known where they were hidden."

"Is Baron Woodhouse willing to prosecute his son for this crime?"

"No. He blames himself for not taking the boy in hand at an earlier age. But upon learning of this latest infamy, the baron had no choice but to take legal measures to disown his youngest son and cut off the allowance he had settled on him. Young Woodhouse is without a feather to fly with, and he dares not return to the Lake District for fear those holding his vouchers will exact their revenge."

Vanessa leaned back in her chair. She was feeling lightheaded. "This is even worse than I could have imagined. I must tell Millie."

"Yes, she must be told." Charles nodded. "I could tell her, if you wish."

Vanessa took a deep calming breath and squared her shoulders. "Thank you, Charles. It is kind of you to offer, but I think it would be better coming from me. I suspect once Millie hears Mr. Woodhouse is a scoundrel, she will be quite embarrassed. I do not believe she would want either you or Aunt Lolly to know she had been so mistaken in her judgment."

"No doubt you are right. It is kind of you to attempt to save Millie embarrassment."

Charles took her hand and Vanessa's brows rose in surprise. His grip was much stronger than it had been before. "Your hand is much improved."

"Yes, and my leg has regained some measure of strength. I can now walk for short distances with only the aid of my cane."

"Why did you not tell me before?"

Charles laughed. "I wished to surprise you. Cousin Camilla and I have been practicing your exercises each evening while you partake of the pleasures of society with my wife."

"You have lifted my spirits." Vanessa stood up and dropped a kiss upon the top of his head.

"That is what I intended. You have a difficult task before you. I do not believe our Millie shall like the news you must give her."

"No, indeed not." Vanessa sighed. "But you have made this day brighter. For that I thank you."

"And I thank you for all you have done for me. But I must ask you to keep the secret of my partial recovery for a bit longer."

"Of course." Vanessa smiled. "But why do you wish such good news to remain a secret?"

Charles laughed and an impish twinkle appeared in his eye. "I want to surprise my dear wife."

* * *

Though the prospect of facing Millie with what they had uncovered about Mr. Woodhouse was daunting, Vanessa had not even thought to shirk the task.

She found Millie in their sitting room and conveyed the contents of the letter calmly, expecting that her charge would break down in tears. Instead, Millie's composure had not shattered in the slightest as Vanessa listed the full extent of Mr. Woodhouse's transgressions.

"Are you quite through?"

Millie's light blue eyes held a hard gleam and her words were calm and measured.

"Yes, that is all." Vanessa reached for Millie's hand but Millie pulled back. "I know that this cannot be easy for you, and I do wish it had not been necessary to tell you."

"No doubt you do."

Vanessa frowned as Millie's puzzling reaction began to come clear. "Do you disbelieve me? I have the letter from Lord Treverton's agent, if you should care to read it yourself."

"Oh, I believe you. I have no doubt his agent wrote those very words. But he is mistaken."

"Mistaken? How could he be mistaken? He spoke with the baron himself."

Millie's blazed with anger. "The baron himself is mistaken and should be punished for spreading such tales about his son. Woody has told me all about it, so you needn't presume you can pull the wool over my eyes."

"What, precisely, has Mr. Woodhouse told you?" Vanessa experienced a sinking feeling as she gazed into Millie's uncompromising eyes. Had Millie gulped down this scoundrel's story hook, line, and sinker?

"Woody knew you would try to discredit him and he prepared me by arming me with the truth. We have discussed all his problems, and he is not to blame for any of them."

Vanessa knew she would get nowhere if she argued with Millie. Mr. Woodhouse had coached her too well. Instead, she did her best to assume a reasonable tone. "You must tell me what he said. If, as you claim, the accusations in this letter are naught but a pack of lies, your Mr. Woodhouse has a powerful enemy."

"Yes, you are right." Millie seemed somewhat taken aback. "Even Woody's own father believes the lies."

"It appears all opinion is against Mr. Woodhouse, even that of his own blood. This is very serious, Millie."

"Yes." Millie frowned. "But why are you concerned? Woody has told me you do not care for him."

"I do not know him sufficiently well to make a judgment in the matter. But I would like to know the truth about Mr. Woodhouse. It is never right to accuse someone falsely."

"I told Woody you would be fair." Millie gave a decisive nod. "Woody said if you heard the lies being bandied about, you would forbid me from seeing him. You will not do that, will you, Vanessa?"

"Not as long as they are lies."

"They are! I am convinced they are!" Millie twisted her fingers together in her lap. "I wish I could tell you how untrue they are, but I have promised Woody not to betray his confidence. The things they say are so awful. How can they do this to him?"

Vanessa hesitated, quickly deciding upon a course of action. "I do not know. But I must ask you, do you still love Mr. Woodhouse?"

"Yes, with all my heart. It pains me that Woody is under such a dark cloud of suspicion when he has done nothing to warrant it."

It was time to play her trump card. Vanessa hated duplicity in any form, but Millie was far too emotional to listen to reason. "If you love Mr. Woodhouse as you say you do, you must endeavor to clear his name."

"Yes, indeed I shall!" Millie gave her a radiant smile. "The moment we are wed, I plan to use my marriage settlement to buy up all his vouchers."

Vanessa struggled to remain calm. It was worse than she suspected. Millie would give her wealth over with a glad heart, never doubting the veracity of Mr. Woodhouse's words. "But that will not serve. You must clear his name *before* you are wed."

"Before? But why, Vanessa?"

"No one will believe a wife. It is her duty to uphold her husband's name. Though I do not approve of such actions, it is quite common for a wife to lie to protect her husband's interests."

"Yes." Millie nodded thoughtfully. "That is quite true."

Vanessa pressed her advantage. "And if you marry Mr. Woodhouse before his name has been cleared, all will accuse him of duping you. That would add another false charge to his slate."

"What would you advise me to do?"

Vanessa smiled. She had won this round, at least. "You must tell me the truth about Mr. Woodhouse so I can aid you in clearing his name. Once Stephen and I are convinced Mr. Woodhouse is an honorable gentleman, none shall dare doubt our opinion."

"I must think on this for a moment. If it were my secret, I would gladly tell you. Woody has begged me to keep his troubles private, and I have given my word to do so. I should not like to break my promise to him."

"Of course not. But you must think of the greater good. Buying up Mr. Woodhouse's vouchers will end his debt, but his name will still be under a cloud. Do you wish him to struggle under false suspicions the rest of his life?"

"You know I do not!"

"Then tell me what Mr. Woodhouse has imparted to

you. I shall never let on I know, and we shall work together to clear his name. You trust me, do you not?"

"I never doubted you, Vanessa, not even for a moment." Tears gathered in Millie's eyes. "And I felt so dreadful about deceiving you I could barely live with myself. When Woody confided in me, I wanted to tell you immediately. But poor Woody does not trust anyone now his own father has betrayed him. I could not convince him to trust you."

"That is quite understandable. It is not an easy thing to trust again, once one's trust has been betrayed."

Millie leaned forward, reaching out for Vanessa's hand. "You will not betray our trust, will you?"

"No, I will not." Vanessa vowed to give no promise she could not keep. "If what Mr. Woodhouse has told you is truth, I shall spare no effort to assist you in clearing his name."

"And you will convince Stephen to approve our match?"

Vanessa hoped her promise would not come back to haunt her. "If the charges against Mr. Woodhouse are false and every word he has spoken to you is truth, I shall urge Stephen to accept his suit for your hand."

"You are wonderful. You have always been and ever shall be my dearest friend."

"And you will be mine." Vanessa smiled at her. "And now you must make me a promise."

"What is that?"

Millie looked a bit fearful and Vanessa smiled to set her at ease. "You must not confess to Mr. Woodhouse what you have told me. I should not like to raise false hopes until there is cause for him to celebrate. Will you promise me that?"

"Oh, yes!" The concerned expression on Millie's face disappeared in a trice. "I do not want to tell him, either. I should *never* like him to know I broke his confidence."

"Good. It is our secret then. Now let us go through these charges against your Mr. Woodhouse one by one so you may tell me precisely what he said to explain them."

Eighteen

Vanessa sat at her dressing table while Colette arranged her hair for the evening. Since she had already enlisted the abigail's aid in watching Millie, and it was clear Colette shared Vanessa's concerns, Vanessa had told her how she had confronted Millie with the contents of the letter Lord Treverton had received from his agent.

"And Miss Millie refused to believe it." Colette smoothed the brush over Vanessa's short hair.

"Indeed, she did." Vanessa was amazed at her abigail's prescience. "How did you know her reaction?"

"I suspected the scoundrel had taken pains to bias Miss Millie against the charges leveled against him."

"You are quite correct." Vanessa smiled, noting Colette had taken to calling Mr. Woodhouse *the scoundrel.* "Mr. Woodhouse fabricated a lie to cover each and every accusation."

"What of the squire's young daughter? Did the scoundrel deny that?"

Vanessa laughed bitterly. "Indeed, he did. He told Millie the girl found herself increasing after a dalliance with one of her father's grooms. When she confessed this to the squire and pleaded for his help, the two of them hatched a plot to force Mr. Woodhouse to marry her."

"A convenient excuse and one we cannot prove false, since only the girl and that scoundrel know what transpired between them." Colette sighed. "What of the gambling and his many vouchers?"

"Mr. Woodhouse lays the blame for that at the squire's door. He told Millie the squire and his daughter started rumors about his gambling so Baron Woodhouse would disown him and he would have to marry the girl."

"Very clever. And the gang of thieves?"

"He claims it was yet another rumor the squire and his daughter used to discredit him. He has sworn to Millie he had no part in the thievery."

Colette put down the brush with a bit more force than was necessary. "And Miss Millie believes his excuses?"

"She accepts every word as truth. Millie thinks Mr. Woodhouse was quite correct in fleeing the situation. After they marry, they intend to return to the Lake District on their wedding trip. Once there, Millie will buy up the forged vouchers the squire and his daughter have scattered throughout the countryside, and then they shall attempt to make peace with the baron."

"*Merci!*" Colette sighed deeply. "Miss Millie is a true innocent to believe such a Banbury tale!"

"Yes, she is. She is convinced Mr. Woodhouse did not debauch the squire's daughter, drink strong spirits to excess, or conspire to steal from his family estate, and she is equally convinced Mr. Woodhouse does not engage in games of chance. It seems he has taken a solemn vow never to do so, and Millie has accepted his word on the matter."

"Miss Millie is naïf." Colette sighed. "Perhaps the scoundrel will be able to hold off gambling for a time, but he shall soon slip back. A leopard cannot change his spots."

"That is my hope, Colette, and we must pray Mr. Woodhouse does so before he succeeds in becoming Millie's husband. We must also pray Millie will see evidence of Mr. Woodhouse's wrongdoing with her own eyes."

There was a scratching on the door, and Colette rushed to open it. When she returned, she held a message that she quickly passed to Vanessa. "This letter has just arrived for you. The footman said it was delivered by someone wearing Lord Holmsby's livery."

"Perhaps it is good tidings." Vanessa unfolded the paper and scanned the lines quickly. When she looked up, she was smiling. "Mr. Woodhouse has asked Lord Holmsby to meet him at *The Black Queen.*"

Colette's eyes widened. *"The Black Queen?* Even I have heard of this place. It is a notorious gambling hell."

"Yes, indeed." Vanessa smiled at her shocked abigail. "And why would Mr. Woodhouse go there, if not to gamble?"

"Then you will tell Miss Millie of this message?"

"It would do little good to *tell* her. I plan to present this evidence so as to leave no doubt of Mr. Woodhouse's infamy."

"What could be keeping Woody?" Millie whispered behind her fan as she turned to gaze at the doorway of Lady Pierpont's drawing room. She had done so at least a dozen times in the past hour.

"Are you certain he intended to be present?" Vanessa used her fan also, to cover her action from the singer who was performing.

"He promised me he would. It is not like Woody to fail to keep his word."

"Perhaps he has been unavoidably delayed." Vanessa patted Millie's hand, wondering what her young charge would do when the full extent of Mr. Woodhouse's duplicity became known.

Another few moments passed and the soprano finished her piece. There were audible sighs of relief from the lords and ladies in attendance as she resumed her chair, and Vanessa was thankful Aunt Lolly had chosen to remain at home. No doubt she would have developed a headache before the first performance ended.

Their hostess, Lady Pierpont, rose from her chair and smiled at the assemblage. "Let us pause for refreshments at this time. When our brief intermission has concluded, I shall present you with a delightful surprise. I have persuaded my dear daughter, Miss Penelope Pierpont, to perform for our pleasure."

There was a round of polite applause and the guests rose to their feet. When the ladies seated nearest them had vacated their chairs, Millie turned to Vanessa. "I do hope Lady Pierpont's daughter is not a soprano."

"No, I understand Miss Pierpont performs upon the harp."

"Then perhaps that will not be so dreadful." Millie's lips turned up in a slight smile. "I do believe one more high note would have given me the headache."

"That is quite understandable. I feel the same. Let us avail ourselves of some lemonade. I am quite parched."

"Would you fetch one for me also?" Millie gazed up at her, pleadingly. "I do not wish to leave for fear I shall miss Woody when he arrives."

"Of course." Vanessa rose from her chair and set off before Millie could change her mind. She had been wishing to speak to Lord Holmsby and had spotted him in the small audience. Millie could not have given her a better opportunity, and she intended to take full advantage of it.

It appeared Lord Holmsby had been wishing to speak to Vanessa, as well, for she found him pacing the corridor outside the door, waiting for her.

"John." Vanessa smiled at him. "I am very glad you are here."

Lord Holmsby nodded and took her arm. "And I was

hoping I would have the opportunity to speak with you in private."

"Let us waste no further time, then." Vanessa gestured toward a bench at the far end of the corridor. "I do believe we should be quite private if we walked to that bench."

Lord Holmsby drew her away from the crowd, and they arrived at the bench in short order. He waited until she was seated and then sat beside her. "You received my message?"

"Yes. I plan to take Millie to *The Black Queen* this evening, immediately following Lady Pierpont's entertainment."

"You cannot do that!" Lord Holmsby was clearly shocked. "*The Black Queen* is not the sort of locale polite ladies frequent. You would both be in grave danger if you appeared in such a notorious gambling hell."

"I know that, John, and I have taken the necessary precautions. Lord Treverton's coachman and his brother have agreed to accompany us. Once Millie has seen Mr. Woodhouse, we shall depart with the utmost haste."

"You do not understand. Once inside, you will have no opportunity to depart. *The Black Queen* is no gentlemen's club. Any lady who ventures through the door is thought to be fair game by the band of cutthroats and cardsharps who frequent the place."

Vanessa's eyes widened and she shivered slightly. "It is so bad as that?"

"It is worse. I cannot let you take Millie there. It would be unconscionable of me."

"But we must go. If we do not, Millie will insist upon marrying Mr. Woodhouse. We cannot permit her to make such a dreadful mistake."

"No, we cannot. I must make a plan then, and quickly. Is there to be a second intermission?"

"Yes. Aunt Lolly told me Lady Pierpont always has two

intermissions, one for liquid refreshment only and a second for a more substantial repast."

"I promise I shall have all at the ready before the second intermission has concluded. Can you convince Millie to leave?"

"I am certain she would be delighted to leave. She already chomps at the bit. All it should take is one more untalented soprano before she will be more than willing to leave. Are you certain Mr. Woodhouse will be at *The Black Queen?*"

"He is there now and has no plans to leave. I promised him I would come immediately after Lady Pierpont's entertainment, and he assured me he will wait for me."

"He is gambling?"

"And losing." Lord Holmsby wore an expression of disgust. "Perhaps it was not entirely proper of me, but I told my man to advance him enough blunt to keep him at the tables until I return."

"That was devilishly clever of you. I shall enjoy matching wits with you once you become Millie's husband."

"How very kind you are to carry us home, Lord Holmsby." Millie gave him a radiant smile. "Lord Treverton's coach was not due to arrive until Lady Pierpont's entertainment had concluded, and I must admit I could not bear another note of music."

"Nor I." Vanessa winked at Lord Holmsby as she was assisted inside his comfortable coach.

"What of Miss Pierpont?" Lord Holmsby entered the coach and took a seat next to Millie. "I heard she was quite adept at the harp."

Millie giggled. "Adept? Whoever told you that had no ear for music, Lord Holmsby."

"Now that I think on it, I do believe it was her mother." Lord Holmsby chuckled and signaled his driver to spring the horses. "Would you ladies object if we took a slight detour so I may make a brief stop?"

Vanessa shook her head quickly, before Millie could think to object. "Not at all, Lord Holmsby. We are far ahead of our schedule as it is. Lady Pierpont's musicale will not conclude for at least another hour."

"Excellent. I shall have you safely at home long before Lord Treverton's coachman is prepared to set out to fetch you. You need have no worry on that score. And you are perfectly safe with me."

"We did not doubt it, even for a moment." Millie smiled up at him.

As Millie and Lord Holmsby began to converse, Vanessa leaned back against the squabs. She felt perfectly safe with John and she had noticed that in addition to his driver, he carried along two others of his employ. The driver was large and burly; the other two servants were of like build. If they encountered any adversity, Vanessa had no doubt John and his men would protect them.

Vanessa closed her eyes and gave a small prayer that their effort to show Millie the truth about Mr. Woodhouse would be successful. She was curious about how John intended to accomplish this deed, but she could not inquire without alerting Millie.

When she opened her eyes again, Vanessa noticed the interior of John's coach was luxurious. If Millie accepted his suit and became his wife, she would lack for nothing wealth could buy. She would not lack for affection, either, if the look in John's eyes was any indication. He gazed at Millie with fondness as she chattered on about the sights they had seen and the balls they had attended.

Vanessa reached up and pulled aside the curtain slightly. They were nearing a more disreputable part of the city, with streets that were narrow and filled with debris. She spotted a man leaning against a lamppost, hugging the base to keep his balance. No doubt he was suffering from the ill effects of strong drink, as his clothing was rumpled and his hat was askew.

Another group of men on a corner caught Vanessa's eye. They looked to be ruffians, and one had a scar running the length of his cheek. They looked up as the carriage passed them and Vanessa shivered slightly, thankful she had not ventured into this area alone. John had been quite correct. These were not the proper environs for a lady.

As Vanessa watched, the coach slowed and pulled up before a disreputable building. Several men near the door appeared to be guarding the place.

She glanced over at John and he gave a slight nod. They had arrived at *The Black Queen*. Vanessa nodded back and took a deep breath for courage. What transpired during the next few minutes would decide Millie's future happiness.

Millie ceased her chattering as the coach came to a halt. She pulled aside the curtain, took one peek out the window, and turned to Lord Holmsby in alarm. "Why are we stopping *here*?"

"I must go inside for a moment." Lord Holmsby took her hand. "Do not leave the coach for any reason. I shall be back in a trice. You and Miss Holland will be perfectly safe with my men to guard you."

Millie began to frown. "But where are we, Lord Holmsby? This place looks disreputable."

"It is called *The Black Queen,* and you are quite right, Lady Thurston. It is one of London's most notorious gambling hells."

Millie appeared alarmed by this news and she turned to Lord Holmsby, shocked. "And you are going inside?"

"Yes. An acquaintance of mine is here this evening, and I must speak to him for a moment. You also know him, and I shall endeavor to bring him out and convince him to return home."

"I see." Millie nodded. "It is good of you to attempt to remove your acquaintance from these unsavory premises."

"Thank you, Lady Thurston. And now, if you ladies will excuse me, I shall go and make my effort. Peek out from behind the curtains if you must, but take care not to be seen. No doubt our mutual acquaintance would be overset if he knew you had witnessed his fall from propriety."

John had told Millie just enough of the truth to pique her curiosity, but he had not alerted her to the fact Mr. Woodhouse was inside.

Once he had climbed out of the coach and shut the door securely behind him, Millie turned to Vanessa with unabashed interest. "Lord Holmsby said we knew this unfortunate gentleman. My guess is it is Mr. Palmer. Woody said he often indulges in games of chance."

"Perhaps you are correct."

"Or could be Lord Donlevy. His sister told me he used to gamble away his allowance within a week of receiving it. Of course, that was when he was at Cambridge. I do not know if he has continued the practice."

Vanessa could hold her peace no longer. Guilt assailed her and she frowned slightly. "What if the gentleman is Mr. Woodhouse?"

"Woody?" Millie's brows shot up with surprise. "No, Vanessa, most assuredly not. I know you still have reservations, but you shall see you are quite wrong."

It seemed nothing would shake Millie's faith save seeing Mr. Woodhouse's perfidy with her own eyes. "I do hope it is not. I know you hold him in great affection, and I should not like to see you disappointed."

"I will not be disappointed." Millie's chin lifted slightly. "And once you see dear Woody is not the gentleman Lord Holmsby seeks to rescue, I would hope you will extend even greater efforts to clear his name."

"If that is the case, I shall do precisely that." Vanessa

made the promise with an uneasy heart, wondering what she would do if John could not bring Mr. Woodhouse from the premises. Coming here tonight had been a great risk. If Mr. Woodhouse had decided to leave, Millie would never believe he had been here in the first place.

"Look, Vanessa." Millie pulled the curtain aside slightly and peeked out. "Someone is coming out."

Vanessa lifted her curtain and watched the doorway. "Yes, indeed. I do believe it is Lord Holmsby, and there is another gentleman and a lady behind him."

"A lady, Vanessa?" Millie gave a short laugh. "She is most certainly not a *lady*! All one need do is observe her to arrive at that conclusion."

Millie was quite right. The woman in question wore a gown that would have put any true lady to the blush, and the way she held her escort's arm, pressing her body closely against his and laughing raucously left little doubt her virtue and her favors had a price.

Millie shivered. "How can she debase herself in this way? And the gentleman she partners is no better. He should be thoroughly ashamed of his actions."

"Indeed, he should be." Vanessa watched from her peephole, willing John to entice the couple further into the street so their faces were exposed by the light.

"I cannot recognize him. His face is still in the shadows." Millie lowered her voice to a whisper as Lord Holmsby and the couple drew nearer to the coach. "I do hope Lord Holmsby does not expect us to share the coach with this rogue."

"I am certain he does not." Vanessa reached out for Millie's hand. In only a matter of moments, the gentleman's face would be visible.

As they watched, Lord Holmsby reached into his pocket and drew out some blunt. He moved closer to the carriage lamps to count it out. The gentleman followed him.

"He has his back to us, but he seems quite familiar," Millie whispered. "If only he would turn around."

At that precise instant, Lord Holmsby moved, drawing the gentleman into the circle of light. Millie gave a shocked gasp as she recognized Mr. Woodhouse. She turned to Vanessa, an expression of stunned disbelief on her face. "Vanessa! It is Woody!"

"I fear it is." Vanessa gathered the quaking girl into her arms.

"There must be some explanation. Perhaps he came to rescue a friend, or . . . or perhaps that awful woman is a relative he seeks to save from her horrible and degrading life. That must be it. Woody gave me his vow he would never gamble!"

"Hush, dear." Vanessa put her finger over Millie's lips. "They are speaking. Let us listen, and perhaps your hopes will be borne out."

Mr. Woodhouse turned to smile at his companion, fondling her in a most shocking manner. "C'mon, Lizzie. I'll win back the blunt I lost, and then we'll go back to your room."

"You are so sweet, Woody." The woman reached up to run her fingers through his hair. "And you'll give me a present after?"

Mr. Woodhouse nodded. " 'Course I will. I always do, don't I?"

"Just a moment, Woodhouse." Lord Holmsby took his arm. "Perhaps it would be best if you leave off gambling for the night."

"Leave off?" Mr. Woodhouse staggered a bit as he turned toward Lord Holmsby. Both Millie had Vanessa could see he was quite foxed. "I had a run of bad luck, but that's about to change, now that I've got my lucky lady with me. Right, Lizzie?"

"Whatever you say, Woody." The woman giggled and patted the side of his face.

"Lemme go, Holmsby." Mr. Woodhouse shook off Lord Holmsby's restraining hand, almost losing his balance in the process. "They're savin' my place for me. Can't say as I trust 'em. Don't wanna give 'em time to stack the deck."

"One moment, Woodhouse. I cannot make you another loan. If you lose the stake I have provided, the well has dried up."

"Your well don't matter, Holmsby." Mr. Woodhouse gave a most unpleasant chuckle. "I got my own well waitin' for me, soon as I marry Millie."

The woman began to giggle. "Millie? Is that the little chit that's going to make us rich, Woody?"

"Right you are. She's the daughter of an earl and as rich as Golden Ball. It won't be long now, Lizzie. Once I marry Millie, you and I will be swilling down champagne and living the high life."

John stepped closer. For a moment, Vanessa thought he might plant the rogue a facer. But he drew back at the last moment and managed to control his ire. "This is a warning, Woodhouse. Do not mention the young lady's name in that manner again. And never speak of her here."

"So that's the way the wind blows." Mr. Woodhouse gave a nasty chuckle. "You're out of luck, Holmsby. The chit's mine for the taking and I won't lose her to the likes of you. And if you're thinking to tell her you spotted me here, it won't do you a parcel of good. She'll just think you're jealous and refuse to believe you."

Vanessa leaned forward to take Millie's hands as the girl began to shiver uncontrollably. "I know what pain this has caused you, but you must be thankful you have learned the truth."

Millie raised stricken eyes to her. "My heart is truly broken. And I am so ashamed I let that . . . that scoundrel dupe me. How could I have placed my faith in him when you attempted to warn me away? I should have trusted you. And I should have seen him for the blackguard he is. Lord Holmsby must think I am horribly hen-witted!"

Vanessa held Millie's hands and squeezed them tightly. "I am certain he does not. He regards you as a charming innocent, and that is precisely what you are. You were taken in by Mr. Woodhouse, true, but it is not at all uncommon for a young lady to be misled by a rogue."

"Then you do not think that Lord Holmsby will think less of me for my mistake?"

"No, dear." Vanessa smiled. Perhaps Millie's heart would not be broken for long if she was already thinking of the impression she had made upon John. "I daresay Lord Holmsby will think even more of you. Your loyalty to Mr. Woodhouse was not shaken until you viewed his misdeeds with your own eyes. Such loyalty is admirable, even though it was misplaced. I would hope you have the courage to thank Lord Holmsby for his efforts to spare you from making a disastrous mistake."

After a few more moments, Lord Holmsby returned to the coach. Once they were under way, he turned to Millie with concern. "You must accept my apologies, Lady Thurston. It was not my intention to make you suffer such a distressing ordeal. I had thought only to show you Woodhouse was here."

"I know." Millie took his arm. "But you were right, Lord Holmsby. I would not have believed it if I had not seen it for myself. And I thank you for sparing me what would have been even greater distress."

Lord Holmsby nodded. "You have great courage, Lady Thurston."

"And great naivete, I fear." Millie managed a small sad smile. "I truly did not believe Mr. Woodhouse was capable of such duplicity."

"Nor did I. He duped us all, Lady Thurston. He also fooled me for a time."

"He did?" Millie's eyes widened in surprise. "But you

are so sophisticated, Lord Holmsby. Surely you were not misled for long."

Lord Holmsby chuckled, covering Millie's hand with his own. "For much longer than I should have liked. He played the part well, and it is no wonder he deceived us. I have only one more comment I wish to make on the matter, if you will give me leave."

"I will." Millie nodded quickly.

"I shall do all in my power to see no one hears of this regrettable incident. Woodhouse did not guess you and Miss Holland were hidden in my coach. He has no inkling he was observed, and I assure you my employees can be trusted not to carry tales."

Millie shivered slightly. "Then I must ask your advice, Lord Holmsby, for I find myself in a dreadful quandary."

"I shall be delighted to assist you in any manner you deem advisable. I wish only for your happiness and well being."

"Thank you." Millie appeared truly grateful. "It is Mr. Woodhouse. If what you have said is correct and he does not know I am on to him, he will assume I shall receive him with the same . . . the same affection I previously held for him. No doubt he will attempt to call upon me in the very near future. I must confess I do not know how I should proceed."

Lord Holmsby nodded. "I had not thought of that, but you are right. Woodhouse will assume he still enjoys your good graces. Let me think on this for a moment."

Vanessa held her breath as John mulled over the dilemma. She had a perfect solution to Millie's problem, but she would let John offer it.

"I know it is indelicate of me to ask, but I must know before I give you my answer." Lord Holmsby took Millie's hands in his. "Have you made any promises to Woodhouse?"

Millie frowned slightly, but then shook her head. "He

spoke often of our marriage, but I am certain I made no promises. Perhaps he had reason to assume I would accept his proposal, but I did not actually tell him I would."

"Good. Then it is quite simple. You shall simply find you prefer another gentleman. Woodhouse cannot object, for he has not yet tendered his declaration. It is not unusual for a debutante to change her escort several times of a Season. Indeed, it is quite the thing for a popular young lady to do."

"I agree such a plan would work, but"—Millie paused—"I have no other gentleman to be my escort."

"I am quite willing to be your escort—more than willing, in fact. If you agree, I shall be the first caller to arrive and the last to leave."

"But I cannot ask you to do me such a service." Millie frowned. "It is truly an imposition."

Lord Holmsby chuckled. "Nonsense! It shall be my pleasure. I find your company most charming. All you need do is refuse to see Woodhouse unless I am by your side."

"Yes. And I thank you for offering your protection. I only wish I could be of equal value to you."

"Will you join me for the promenade tomorrow, after your callers have departed? I have a new curricle and team I should like to show to you."

"The promenade?" Millie drew in her breath, and Vanessa could tell she was most pleased. "That is in no way a return of your favor, Lord Holmsby, for I have never taken part in the promenade and have wished to do so. You must think of some other favor I am able to perform for you."

John nodded. Though she could not see it, Vanessa was certain his eyes were sparkling. "I have it, then. Will you allow me to escort you to the Valentine's Day Ball?"

"I shall, with pleasure." Millie smiled as she accepted. "I shall accept any invitation you care to tender."

Lord Holmsby chuckled. "You are charmingly naive, Lady Thurston. What if I should invite you to all future entertainments of the Season?"

"Then I should accept, of course." Millie gave a small giggle, and Vanessa's eyebrows shot up. Her heart appeared to have mended quite miraculously under John's light banter.

"And shall we make a pact not to mention Woodhouse's name in future?"

"A most worthy pact." Millie's voice shook slightly. Perhaps she was not as recovered from her ordeal as she would like to be. "I agree, Lord Holmsby."

Lord Holmsby clearly heard the quiver in Millie's voice, for he reached for a lap robe and tucked it securely around her. "You are cold, my dear. Close your eyes and lean back against the squabs. You are quite safe with me, and I shall have you home in no time at all."

Millie did as he asked, and before many more corners had been turned, she was fast asleep, her breathing deep and even. And then her head slipped closer and closer toward John until she found comfort cushioned against his side. Vanessa smiled at the young couple, so obviously right for each other. And then she sighed, wishing her own problems with Stephen could be settled so easily.

Nineteen

Lolly walked into her husband's study and smiled as she saw him studying a sheaf of papers at his desk. He had taken charge of his estates once more, and it was gratifying to see him hard at work, accomplishing the tasks she had despaired he would ever manage again. She owed a debt of gratitude to Vanessa, for Lolly had never dared hope Charles would progress so far in so little time.

"Good morning, my darling." Charles looked up from his papers to greet her. "I am glad you are here, for there is something I must discuss with you."

Lolly took a seat in the chair that faced her husband's desk. Her hands trembled slightly and she clasped them tightly together on her lap, where he could not see them. This matter he had mentioned must be quite serious, as he was now regarding her with concern. "What is it, Charles?"

"I am concerned over Vanessa. It has been nearly a week since Millie discovered the truth about that young pup Woodhouse, and she seems in better spirits than our Vanessa."

Lolly smiled. She did not wish to discuss Vanessa's brown study, as she was convinced she had guessed the reason for her ill spirits. But discussing Millie's new happiness would be a pleasure. "I daresay Millie is in love, dear, and with the right gentleman this time. She appears most enamored of

Lord Holmsby, and I am convinced the sentiment is mutual."

"Then she has succeeded in banishing Woodhouse from her life?"

"Yes, indeed. She is made of sterner stuff than I had believed possible. Millie's heart was broken, I have no doubt of that, but she has shown great courage in cutting off all ties to that despicable cad."

"And how was this accomplished?"

"With great dispatch, Charles. I daresay Wellington himself would be impressed with the plan Millie hatched up with Lord Holmsby."

"She did not confront young Woodhouse with the evidence of his wrongdoing?"

"No, Millie was convinced he would only offer up another lie to explain the matter, and she did not wish to hear it. With Lord Holmsby's assistance, our Millie set out to convince all in the *ton* she had no quarrel with Mr. Woodhouse, but was much more inclined toward Lord Holmsby." Lolly laughed, reaching out to pat her husband's hand. "And though it may have been a clever ruse in the very beginning, it has now become true."

"Millie has tumbled into love with Lord Holmsby."

"And he has tumbled into love with her. It is quite clear, Charles."

"It could not be simple gratitude on Millie's part? After all, Holmsby saved her from a life of misery."

"No." Lolly shook her head. "It is an emotion far stronger than gratitude. I am convinced Millie has given Lord Holmsby her heart."

"I pray you are right, Lolly. Millie could not find a finer young gentleman. He dropped by to see me yesterday and we had a most enjoyable discussion."

"This is the first I have heard of it." Lolly's eyebrows shot up in surprise. "And you received him, Charles?"

"Of course, my dear. I was most impressed with his

character. I was acquainted with his father before him, and I judge young Holmsby to be an equally honorable gentleman. Do you suspect a declaration is forthcoming?"

"I do." Lolly smiled. "They are so in love, Charles, that they remind me of us. I suspect Lord Holmsby waits only for Stephen to return to make a formal declaration for Millie."

"And Stephen will give his blessing?"

"He would be a fool if he did not. It is one of the most perfect matches that I have ever seen."

"Even more perfect than ours?"

Lolly laughed. She knew she was blushing just remembering how enamored they had been at the start. "Very few couples are as lucky as we have been. My love for you grows stronger with each passing year."

"And mine for you." Charles returned her smile, and they sat in companionable silence for a moment. Then his expression sobered and he frowned again. "You have rather adroitly avoided my initial question. What ails Vanessa? You cannot deny she is not her usual self."

Lolly sighed. She had not wished to explore this subject, but it seemed Charles would not be denied. "No. I cannot deny it. Vanessa has been blue-deviled of late."

"And what do you believe is the cause of her malady?"

Lolly clasped her hands tightly. She could not lie to her husband, but perhaps she could put him off. "I can only speculate, dear, and my speculations are often wrong."

"Come now, Lolly. When have you ever been wrong? You are an excellent judge of character."

Lolly winced. They were venturing into deep waters, and she had a secret she must keep. It would not do for Charles to know the full extent of her worries over Vanessa. "Perhaps she simply misses the close companionship she was used to enjoy with Millie. Now that Millie is off with Lord Holmsby at every opportunity, Vanessa has been left quite alone. It would not be unusual if she were a bit envious."

"No, my dear, that will not fadge. Our Vanessa does not have an envious bone in her body. I am convinced she is delighted over Millie's good fortune. To accuse her of less would be an undeserved insult. You are evading the real answer to my query, my dear, and I insist you tell me."

Charles had left her with no other recourse than the truth. "I do not wish to upset you, dear, but I believe Vanessa has fallen in love with Stephen. And since she knows full well Stephen has a wife, she has gone into despair."

"Vanessa? And Stephen? Are you certain, Lolly?"

"As certain as a mother can be. And I do feel as if Vanessa is my daughter."

"What of Stephen? Does he return her tender feelings?"

"I believe he does, but both are aware their love is quite hopeless. After all, there is Phoebe to consider."

"Phoebe! She was always one to throw a snag in the rein."

"Please, Charles. You must remain calm." Lolly rose from her chair to take her husband's hand. "The doctors have warned you not to become overset."

Charles patted her hand. "I am perfectly calm, my dear, and I am convinced the doctors are wrong. I have long known there was something havey-cavey regarding Phoebe's disappearance, despite your best efforts to hide it from me. I am much recovered now, and you need no longer fear for my health. Do you not think it would be better if you told me the truth?"

"I cannot tell you!" Lolly's face turned pale. The doctors had been most definite Charles should be spared any distressing news for fear it would bring on another occurrence of his illness. "Please, Charles. Let us not discuss this further."

"We *must* discuss it, my dear. I know you have been deceptive for what you believed would be my own good, but I am quite ready to face this problem directly."

"Are you sure?" Lolly gazed at him closely. What she saw reassured her. His eyes were not blazing with fever, nor were his limbs trembling. He looked quite fit, and she wanted to tell him. She had been carrying this burden for so long.

"I assure you I shall not become ill, and I wish to know the truth about Phoebe. It cannot be any worse than what I have imagined, and hearing it from your lips shall greatly relieve my mind."

"Yes." Lolly nodded. It was time to tell him. The ruse had gone on far too long, and there was no need to carry it further. Charles seemed quite calm, and no one could deny he had recovered a great bit of his former stamina.

"Shall we be seated on the couch?" Charles rose to his feet and took his wife's arm.

Lolly smiled at him. It would be a relief to confess the truth at last. "Let me fetch your cane, dear."

"I have no need of it, Lolly." Charles stayed her with his hand. "It is but a short distance from my desk to the couch. I shall manage quite well without it."

Lolly's eyes widened in pleased surprise as Charles led her to the couch. He was walking steadily without the assistance of his cane. "This is remarkable, Charles. Soon you will be dancing again."

"Perhaps." Charles chuckled as he sank down on the soft cushions with Lolly at his side. "But it shall have to be a *very* slow waltz, and I must spend hours practicing with you before I attempt it."

Lolly smiled, feeling quite giddy. "I should not mind that in the slightest, dear. It has been far too long since I have enjoyed your embrace on the dance floor."

"Yes, it has." Charles looked thoughtful for a moment. Then his face took on resolve. "Lolly dear, I know you regard this as most unpleasant, but tell me precisely what happened with Stephen and Phoebe. It is only right that I know."

Lolly sighed. "Phoebe ran off on her wedding trip, leaving only a note for Stephen."

"On her wedding trip?" Charles sighed and shook his head. "My sympathies lie firmly with Stephen on this score. Phoebe was always regrettably high-strung. No doubt there was another gentleman involved."

Lolly raised her brows in surprise. "Why, yes. Phoebe ran off with an Italian nobleman of highly questionable character. Though Stephen spared no expense to find her, he was unsuccessful."

"What did Phoebe write in her note?"

"Only that she had married him to escape my watchful eye. I fear the blame for this dreadful tangle can be placed directly at my door. I did not think I had supervised Phoebe too closely, but it appears she regarded me as her jailer and used her marriage to Stephen as a means of escape."

"You did not supervise her too closely, Lolly." Charles drew his wife closer to his side. "The very fact Phoebe managed to escape belies that. You say Stephen searched for her?"

Lolly blinked back tears. "He searched for six months, to no avail. He followed every sighting of Phoebe, but arrived too late in every instance. Finally, when he had exhausted all avenues, he returned home to take charge of dear Millie."

"And spread the tale that Phoebe had taken ill on their wedding trip."

"Stephen wished to protect Phoebe and us from malicious gossip."

Charles sighed and shook his head. "Even though

Phoebe had left him, Stephen took all measures to pre-
serve her good name?"

"Yes, and he was successful. To this very day, no one
suspects the story of Phoebe's illness is not true. He has
told no one but me, Charles. Not even Millie knows the
truth."

"But what of the letters Phoebe sent to me? And the
gifts and the miniatures that have arrived throughout the
years?"

"I wrote those letters and sent those gifts to you, and
Stephen hired an artist to paint the miniatures. The doctors told us you could not endure such a shock, and I was
afraid you would die if we told you the truth about your
daughter. I convinced Stephen to perpetuate this ruse,
and he became my willing accomplice."

Charles raised his brows. "Your love for me prompted
you to devise such an elaborate ruse?"

"Of course." Lolly covered his hand with her own. "We
did not want to distress you, and it seemed the only course
to take. And we never stopped trying to find her. Stephen
hired a team of investigators, and we have received word
of her in several different countries. Stephen has gone to
search for her each time he has received a report. We
shall never cease in our efforts to find your daughter, but
I fear there is little hope. Stephen's investigators have
warned him too much time has expired and the trail has
gone cold."

"Yes. That is what my men have told me, as well."

"*Your* men?" Lolly's eyes widened and she turned to
look up at her husband in shock. "You knew?"

Charles smiled. "Yes, my dear. Phoebe was never the
loving daughter you and Stephen have made her out to
be. She was concerned only for herself, and I thought it
most odd of her to write weekly letters or to send thoughtful gifts. You painted it up much too brown, and I became

convinced you and Stephen were hiding the truth from me. I had no choice but to learn it myself."

"Then you knew all along?" Lolly held her breath, waiting for his answer. Had their ruse been so ill conceived from its very conception?

"In the beginning, I was far too ill to think clearly. I have no doubt you and Stephen were right not to tell me. But Vanessa has done wonders to aid in my recovery, and once I could put pen to paper, I began to think clearly about Phoebe's mysterious absence. Once I became convinced there was more to the story, I began to investigate her whereabouts."

Lolly sighed and moved a bit closer to her husband's side. It was a blessed relief to speak candidly. "Your investigators learned she had run off on her wedding trip?"

"Yes, and they described the Italian nobleman's character as most dubious. They also reported he was known to be quite dashing, and I must say I was not as shocked as you suspected I would be. Phoebe always showed a decided tendency to emulate her mother, and perhaps even her father."

Lolly's eyes widened at her husband's words. "Her *father*?"

"I am not Phoebe's father, you see. I did not suspect at the time, but Phoebe's mother confessed her secret to me on her deathbed."

Lolly's mouth opened in surprise, and then she reached out to embrace him tightly. "Oh, Charles! I am so dreadfully sorry. You must have been terribly distressed."

"Yes." Charles's arms tightened around her. "I did not suspect, you see. But my wife wished me to raise Phoebe as my own, and I vowed I would. I made every effort to fulfill that promise, Lolly, never divulging her parentage until this very moment."

"And you have done precisely as you promised, my dear." Lolly gazed at her husband in admiration. Charles was a fine man, and his revelation to her regarding Phoebe confirmed what she had long known of his character.

There was a tap at the door and Charles patted Lolly's hand. "That must be Hodges with the morning post. Will you fetch it from him, my dear?"

"Of course." Lolly rose and opened the study door, taking the stack of letters from Hodges. When she returned to the couch, she handed them to Charles. "We have a whole sheaf of invitations, I see. And there is one letter addressed to you personally."

Charles nodded as he removed the envelope from the stack and opened it. "It is from the investigator I hired, my dear. Shall I read it now?"

"Yes, indeed." Lolly watched the emotions play over her husband's face as he read the letter. She could not help but hope the investigator had learned something new.

"It is most interesting, Lolly." Charles folded the letter and turned to her with a smile. "He shall be here this very afternoon with news of Phoebe that he does not wish to trust to the post. His name is Greaves. Will you make certain he is shown directly to my study when he arrives?"

Lolly nodded. "Of course. I shall greet him myself and bring him to you. And I shall order refreshments for you both."

"For three of us." Charles reached out to take Lolly's hand once more. "Will you join us, Lolly? Now that we know each other's secrets, there is no need for us to hide anything further."

"Indeed, there is not." Lolly reached up to touch her husband's cheek. The old closeness, which she had thought would never blossom between them again, was back in full measure.

"I love you, Lolly."

"And I love you, Charles." Lolly nestled her cheek

against his. She felt a peace within her that made her eyes sparkle, and she knew she had never felt so happy as she did in that moment, knowing her dear husband was truly well and with her once again.

Twenty

Vanessa rushed down the corridor, pinching her cheeks to provide color. All had commented she looked a bit pulled, and she did not want Charles to notice there was anything amiss. Vanessa failed to understand how a broken heart could manifest itself in outward appearance, but it was quite evident her anguish over Stephen had affected her physical well being.

Aunt Lolly had come to Vanessa only moments before and told her Charles requested her presence immediately in his study. She had also said they would take tea together, and though Vanessa was not in the least bit sharp set, she had vowed to eat enough cakes so Charles should not notice her deplorable lack of appetite.

Once she arrived at the study door, Vanessa straightened her gown, fluffed her hair, and tapped softly. At the summons to enter, given in Charles's deep voice, Vanessa took a deep breath and opened the door.

"Vanessa, my dear." Charles smiled and motioned to the chair before his desk. "I have ordered tea for us."

Vanessa smiled. "That was kind of you, Charles. Shall I pour?"

"I believe I can manage quite well." Charles lifted the heavy teapot and poured out two cups. "As you see, my left hand is improving by the day."

Vanessa smiled. "Indeed, it is. You have not spilled a drop."

"Take a cake, Vanessa. Cook has made your favorite lemon seed, and they are still warm from the oven. Lolly has warned me you have lost flesh and we must fatten you up before the Valentine's Day Ball tomorrow."

Vanessa frowned slightly as she took a lemon-seed cake. It was still warm, as Charles had promised, but she knew she could do no more than nibble at it.

"I have a matter of the utmost importance to discuss with you, Vanessa." Charles leaned forward to smile at her. "My man has just left, and he brought me word of Phoebe."

The morsel of cake turned to dust in her mouth and she swallowed hastily. "I hope the countess has recovered from her illness."

"No, dear. I fear she is quite beyond that. My man has just come from Phoebe's grave."

"Her grave?" Vanessa swallowed again. The bite of cake was stuck in her throat, and she took a sip of her tea to wash it down. "I offer my sympathy, Charles, for your loss. I did not know her illness threatened her very life."

"She was never ill, Vanessa. That was the tale Stephen and Lolly concocted to save her reputation from ruin. Phoebe died in Venice, after several nights of drunken revelry, in a carriage accident."

Vanessa's eyes widened and she could not, for the life of her, think of an appropriate comment to make. She just sat there, stunned, holding the cake in her left hand and the teacup in her right.

"I must tell you the whole story, Vanessa, so you will not think ill of Stephen. Will you give me your leave to do so?"

Vanessa nodded, still incapable of speech, and listened as Charles set forth the salient points of the story. When he finished, Vanessa found her hands were shaking uncontrollably, the tea dangerously close to sloshing from her cup. She reached out, set her teacup down on the edge of the desk, and stared at Charles in shock. "The countess ran off immediately following her wedding?"

"That is quite correct, my dear." Charles smiled at her kindly. "And though I should keep this fact from your innocent ears, I must tell you the marriage was never consummated."

A blush crept up Vanessa's neck, and she could feel the heat spread to her cheeks. She remembered Stephen's words to her in the garden—*she never wanted me that way*—and she now understood what he had meant. "Does Stephen know his wife is dead?"

"No. He is still traveling, following another tip he hopes will lead him to Phoebe. But he has promised to return for the Valentine's Day Ball and I have no doubt he shall arrive tonight or early tomorrow."

"And you will tell him then?"

Charles nodded. "I shall inform him he is a widower. And I will pass the word to others as well, telling them of my daughter's death in Italy. I anticipate Stephen will make all haste to offer for you, my dear Vanessa, and I hope you will accept him and become his countess."

"Me?" Vanessa's mouth fell open in shock. "But I cannot marry Stephen."

Charles smiled at her. "It is useless to try to gammon me, my dear. I am sensible of the fact you love Stephen and I am equally certain he loves you in return. And now Phoebe no longer stands in your way . . . "

"No!" Vanessa interrupted him quickly. "It does not make a difference, Charles. I can never marry Stephen."

Charles frowned. "I do not understand, Vanessa. You love Stephen and Stephen loves you. It seems right you should marry."

"No, it would *not* be right."

Charles's frown grew deeper. "Perhaps I have told you too suddenly, and you failed to understand. Phoebe's death has dissolved Stephen's marriage. He is now free to marry you. There is no impediment to your future together."

"But there *is* an impediment." Vanessa raised stricken eyes to Charles. "You do not understand. I would not agree to marry Stephen if he were the last man alive in all of England."

"But why not? It is clear to me you love him."

"Yes, I love him." Vanessa nodded quickly. "But before Stephen left, he . . . he attempted to compromise me in your gardens! And he did not know his wife was dead!"

Charles nodded. "You must forgive him for that, Vanessa. He loves you, my dear, and perhaps he may have gotten a bit ahead of himself, but . . ."

"No!" Vanessa's eyes blazed with reawakened anger. "He attempted to seduce me in his wife's childhood home, under the very noses of her father and stepmother! As much as I still love him, I cannot forgive his licentious behavior."

"Vanessa, dear." Charles reached out, across the top of his desk, for her hand. "Perhaps Stephen's behavior was not all it should be, but he has been under a terrible strain. He has felt it necessary to keep up the appearances of a loving marriage, all the while knowing his wife left him on their wedding trip for another man. Can you not have some sympathy for his predicament?"

Vanessa felt herself beginning to waver, but she straightened her shoulders and shook her head. "No. The circumstances of his marriage are regrettable, but that did not give him license to ask me to be his mistress."

"His behavior was most uncharacteristic." Charles sighed deeply. "I cannot believe that Stephen would offer you such a thing, unless . . ."

Vanessa paled as Charles paused and a thoughtful expression crossed his face. "Unless what, Charles?"

"You must search your heart, Vanessa, and make certain you did not encourage Stephen's advances. If you find you have, you must not place the entire blame upon his shoulders."

Vanessa's heart sank. Charles was right. She had encouraged Stephen by returning his kisses. She gave a small nod and dropped her eyes, a wave of guilt assailing her. "You are right. I did encourage Stephen, and I assure you I feel nothing but shame for my actions. But that does not affect my decision. I still cannot marry Stephen. We have wronged each other, and not even marriage can set that right."

"Are you quite certain, Charles?" Stephen's heart began to pound rapidly in his chest as he faced his father-in-law. His clothing was rumpled and he was weary, but he had not been given the time to change or wash off the dust of his travels. Hodges had insisted Lord Treverton wished to see him the moment he returned.

Charles nodded, pouring out a generous measure of brandy for his son-in-law. "My man has viewed Phoebe's grave, Stephen, and obtained a copy of the official report of her death.

"Poor Phoebe." Stephen sighed as he accepted the brandy and took a restoring swallow. "I bear her no ill will."

Charles frowned. "Perhaps you should. She deceived you from the start and she very nearly ruined you. You cannot deny that."

"No, but Phoebe was a soul in torment. I cannot blame her for something she could not help. She did have her good qualities, Charles, and I am only sorry I was unable to save her from her devils."

Charles sighed. "Phoebe did not wish to be saved, and that is at the crux of this unfortunate matter. I also tried to save her, as did my dear Lolly. But now that Phoebe's brief and painful life is over, it is past time you get on with yours. You are free now, Stephen, from the chains that bound you to Phoebe."

"It seems impossible." Stephen took another sip of his brandy, willing the strong spirits to wash away the bitter taste of ashes in his mouth. "I must go on, of course. But I fear I have made a muddle of my life. My future looks bleak, Charles."

Charles smiled slightly. "Perhaps it is not quite as black as you paint it. If I stood in your boots, Stephen, I should go immediately to the young lady's room and tell her of your love for her. Then I should tender my proposal and spare no effort to convince her to marry me."

"You know?"

Stephen's brows shot upward in surprise, and Charles chuckled at his son-in-law's discomfort. "It would be quite impossible for me *not* to know. I have seen how you moon after her, the very image of a lovesick calf. And she is no better, for she cannot tear her gaze away from yours."

"But that has changed." Stephen sighed. "As I said, I have made a muddle of it."

Charles reached out and poured a bit more brandy into Stephen's snifter. "Perhaps it is not such a terrible muddle as you think. Both Lolly and I have noticed Vanessa has been in the depths of despair since you took your leave. She pecks at her food like a bird, she has dark smudges under her eyes from lack of sleep, and her smiles are seldom and fleeting. I should say, from the benefit of years of experience, Vanessa is deeply in love with you."

"Perhaps she is, but she will not accept my proposal. You do not understand, Charles. I lost control of my emotions, and she will never forgive me that. Even if she could, I will never forget the manner in which I debased her. I offered to take her as my mistress. I shall never forgive myself for that."

Charles began to frown. "So you will not ask her to marry you now that you are free?"

"No." Stephen shook his head, despair welling up in him like a black cloud. "I cannot ask her forgiveness for the very act I cannot forgive in myself. It would not be right, and it would forever come between us. I sought to take full advantage of her tender emotions. By doing so, I have degraded her. I am not worthy to be her husband, and I must give her up."

"But that is ridiculous! It was an error in judgment on your part."

Stephen shook his head, lifting the brandy snifter to his lips and draining it in one long swallow. "I have thought long and hard on this, and I know I am quite correct. I must have no further dealings with Vanessa. I have wronged her, and nothing can set that right."

"You are certain of this?"

Stephen nodded, sighing deeply. "I shall dance with her at the Valentine's Day Ball, as I have promised to do so. But it shall be our last dance together. I shall be eternally grateful to her for saving Millie from Woodhouse's clutches, but after the ball, I shall take my leave and never set eyes on her again."

"So you see, my dear Lolly, they are fools, both of them."

Charles smiled at his wife, who looked lovely in her night rail and wrapper. She had taken to coming in of late to bid him good night, just as she had done in the days before he had been stricken. Of course, things had been very different then. They had shared his bed each night, locked in a warm and loving embrace. Just thinking of it made Charles wish he could turn back the hands of the clock and enjoy the full advantages of their marriage.

"You cannot reason with them?"

Lolly looked anxious, and he pulled her down on the bed beside him, seeking the warm comfort of her arms and her love. "I have made the attempt, and I have failed. They are as stubborn as mules."

"But what shall we do?" Lolly slipped under the covers and moved close to his side. "We must do something. If we let things stay as they are between Vanessa and Stephen, they will be miserable for the remainder of their days."

Charles nodded, slipping his arm around his wife's shoulders. "I know, dear. And I promise you I shall think on it. Perhaps, in the morning, a solution will occur to me."

"At least Millie is happy." Lolly smiled at her husband, reaching up to caress his cheek. "And you say Stephen will accept young Holmsby's offer?"

Charles nodded. "Yes, indeed. He is delighted Woodhouse is out of the picture, and he credits Vannesa for the good deed. He stated he would be eternally grateful to her, but that he could not bear to see her again after the Valentine's Day Ball was concluded."

"He is such a fool!" Lolly shook her head. "Were we that foolish?"

Charles pulled her a bit closer and blessed that fact he had not taken his sleeping draft. "No, dear. Correct me if I am wrong, but I recall only one quarrel before we were wed."

"That is quite correct. But it was a rather large quarrel, Charles. I recall we did not speak for three days."

Charles nodded. "You are quite right. And those three days were almost my undoing. It was such a dreadful quarrel about . . . what *was* it about, Lolly?"

"I do not remember, either." Lolly gave a delighted laugh. "But I do recall it seemed a serious matter at the time. I even thought briefly of crying off."

Charles was surprised. She had never told him this before. "What stopped you, dear?"

"My love for you, of course." Lolly smiled an impish smile. "But another factor also gave me pause."

"And what factor was that?"

"Our engagement notice had already appeared and my mama had sent off the wedding invitations. My temper cooled considerably once I realized I should be required to offer an explanation to all those Mama had invited and pen a retraction to the *Gazette*."

Charles was silent for a long moment. Then he embraced Lolly tightly. "You are a genius, my darling!"

"I am?" Lolly gave him a quizzical look.

"You may have hit upon a way to save Vanessa and Stephen from grief. You said the fact our engagement had been announced gave you pause to reflect before you cried off?"

"Indeed, it did!" Lolly sighed. "I could not help but consider Mama's embarrassment if I did so, and how dreadfully hurt she would be. And then, once my provocation at our quarrel had faded, I realized I did not wish to cry off."

"Perhaps I should announce their engagement, Lolly, in a very public manner."

Lolly looked shocked. "Do you mean to publish it without their knowledge?"

"No." Charles shook his head and a smile hovered about the corners of his mouth. "The ball takes place tomorrow and it is too late to *Gazette* it. I thought, instead, their engagement could be announced at the commencement of our Valentine's Day Ball."

Lolly's mouth opened in amazement and she began to laugh. "You would play such a devious game?"

"I have no other choice. Perhaps they will not go through with the marriage, but my announcement shall force them to speak to each other at the ball, to dance together, and to pretend to the *ton* that they are a loving couple. Who is to say that while discussing how best to extricate themselves from their predicament, they will not work out their differences?"

Lolly thought about what he had said for a long moment. "It is an excellent plan, Charles. I did not know you had it in you to be so diabolically clever. Shall I make the announcement, then?"

"No, my dearest. I shall do it."

"You, Charles?" Lolly's mouth opened in amazement. "But it will mean appearing before the entire *ton!*"

"I know that. Will you remember to tell Yardley to lay out my formal dress?"

"Of course. But . . ." Lolly stopped, clearly unsure what she should say.

Charles smiled at her kindly, knowing full well why she appeared so distressed. "I shall attend the ball and make the announcement of Millie and Holmsby's engagement. I am certain Stephen will accord me that honor. After that announcement has been made, I shall make a second, regarding Vanessa and Stephen's engagement. I am certain neither Stephen nor Vanessa would embarrass me in public by contradicting my words."

"You may be quite certain they will not." Lolly nodded emphatically. But then she reached up to touch his lips. "Have you truly thought on this, Charles? In order for your plan to succeed, you shall have to appear before all of our guests. Are you certain you are willing to make such an announcement?"

Charles smiled. "I am. It is time to set aside my foolish pride. I cannot hide behind closed doors when Vanessa and Stephen's happiness is at stake. And if some are dismayed by my appearance, they are not truly my friends. I am most willing to appear, if you will agree to stay by my side."

"You should not have to ask." Lolly turned her face up to his and kissed him soundly. "I love you with all my heart, my dearest, and I shall always be proud to appear at your side."

Charles smiled, pulling her closer and kissing her soundly upon the lips. Then their kiss deepened and he felt a most welcome response to his wife that he had not experienced for several long and lonely years. "Lolly?"

"Yes, dear."

"We have been apart for far too long." His voice was deep and husky, the voice of a man in love. "Would you care to spend the remainder of this night with me?"

Lolly smiled as she gazed up at him, her love clearly shining in her eyes. "Yes, dearest Charles. I have been dreaming of just such a moment. And if you had not invited me, I would have been forced to play the hoyden and suggest the very same thing!"

Twenty-one

"I have no doubt you shall turn all heads at the ball, Miss Vanessa." Colette stood back to admire her work. "Your gown, it is exquisite!"

Vanessa smiled, taking one last look in the glass. Her deep red ball gown was fetching, and Colette had arranged her hair to perfection, weaving dark red camellias into a floral coronet that was nestled among her shining curls.

"Your will wear your lovely heart pendant this evening?"

Vanessa nodded and stood as still as a statue as Colette hopped up on the chair to fasten the gold chain around her neck. This might be the last time she would wear it, and she knew she would miss its comfort and promise. If her secret admirer appeared at the ball and presented himself to her, Vanessa planned to return the lovely pendant to him and inform him she had given her heart to another. Though his letters to her had been most beautiful and his sentiments had given her spirits a much-needed lift, it would not be fair to encourage his attentions when she was not capable of giving him her love.

Her decision had been reached painfully over the past few days. Vanessa had thought she would be able to put all thoughts of Stephen from her mind, but she could not lay her love to rest so easily. Finally, after hours of inner debate, Vanessa had vowed to remain a spinster, an auntie to all her friends' children and mother to none. She felt it was better not to marry at all, since she could not wed the gentleman who had so completely captured her affections. None would measure up to the love she still felt for the Earl of Bridgeford.

"Perfection!" Colette gained the floor once again and smoothed out Vanessa's skirts. "Miss Millie awaits you in the sitting room. I must say I have never seen her in such lovely form."

Vanessa nodded. "Millie is in love, Colette, and her tender feelings for Lord Holmsby have added to her natural radiance. I saw it myself only this morning, when she came in to tell me Stephen had approved their match."

"Their engagement will be announced tonight at the ball?" Colette smiled in anticipation.

"I have no doubt it will." Vanessa managed what she hoped was a credible smile of her own. Of course she was happy for Millie. That went without saying. But it was difficult to smile in the face of her own disappointment. "Without your watchful presence, Millie might have been duped into running off with the scoundrel. But you held her here until we could expose his true nature, and now dear Millie has found her perfect match. I only wish you could be there to see her first waltz with Lord Holmsby."

Colette blushed a bit at the praise. "I did no more than my duty, Miss Vanessa. And I shall be there to see Miss Millie, along with the rest of the staff. Mr. Yardley has told me of a secret place behind the flowering trees that decorate the interior balcony of the ballroom. We shall all watch Miss Millie waltz with his lordship."

Once Colette had taken her leave, Vanessa picked up her gloves and the lovely ivory fan Aunt Lolly had given her and walked down the corridor to the sitting room. She found Millie perched carefully upon the edge of a chair.

"Millie, you are truly a vision of loveliness." Vanessa smiled at her fondly. Millie was wearing an ice blue confection of satin and lace that set off her dark hair and shining blue eyes to perfection.

"You are in admirable looks, Vanessa." Millie smiled and rose to her feet. "I had thought Aunt Lolly was mistaken when she insisted upon that particular shade of dark red, but it suits you far better than I had dreamed possible."

Vanessa reached out to take Millie's hand. "Thank you, dear Millie. It is difficult to believe you will soon be married with a husband and family of your own. I shall miss our companionship."

"But you shall not miss it." Millie laughed gaily. "The moment we return from our wedding trip, John and I wish you to come and stay with us. There is a lovely dower cottage that we plan to refurbish for you and your papa. All you need do is persuade him to come, and I do not think that will be such a task. I should not like to raise our children without the benefit of your wisdom. Just think of the fun we shall have together, you and your papa and John and me!"

Vanessa had all she could do to maintain her smile. Millie was kind, offering her a lifelong position and a second family to love. It was an offer she would have to regard carefully, and now was not the time to discuss it. Could she convince her papa to leave his home in Bridgeford, where he had spent most of his adult life? It would mean leaving behind dear friends for both of them.

"Say you will come, Vanessa." Millie stared up at her anxiously. "Both John and I have agreed."

Vanessa nodded, squeezing Millie's hand gently. "I shall certainly consider it, dear, but I cannot make a decision of that magnitude lightly. Let us see how we all get on when you come back from your wedding journey. I shall certainly visit you then, if you would like."

"Do you promise?"

"Indeed, I do" Vanessa gave her an encouraging smile. "I should not like to miss all the tales you will tell. I have never traveled, you know, and I have no doubt I shall be fascinated by your descriptions of faraway and exotic places. Once you are settled in your new home, you need only write and I will come to you with the greatest of haste. And now we must hurry, dear, for we have obligations. The hour grows late. Aunt Lolly will become overset if we do not join her in the receiving line."

Vanessa's heart had leaped painfully each time a tall, dark-haired gentleman had appeared in the reception line, but Stephen had not appeared. No doubt he was waiting to greet them in the ballroom, preparing to make the announcement of Millie's engagement to Lord Holmsby.

Alone in her chamber before the ball, Vanessa had decided she would not let on that anything was amiss. She had vowed to behave with the utmost propriety, greeting Stephen politely and pretending all was as it should be. She could only hope Stephen would do the same. It would be difficult, but Vanessa was determined not to allow their quarrel to ruin Millie's evening or become an item of speculation among the members of the *ton*.

"Shall we go in?"

"Yes, Aunt Lolly." Vanessa stepped forward to join Aunt Lolly, who was shepherding Millie and Lord Holmsby toward the door to the ballroom. Aunt Lolly's eyes were sparkling with mirth, and that gave Vanessa pause. She looked a bit like the cat that got into the cream pot. "Is something wrong, Aunt Lolly?"

"Wrong?" Aunt Lolly shook her head. "I should say all is quite right on this evening. You must have faith, my dearest."

Vanessa was considering that puzzling reply when she heard a sound behind her. When she turned, she saw the Bath chair was being wheeled up to join them and her eyes widened in surprise. "Aunt Lolly, Charles is here!"

"Yes, my dear. It is his first public appearance, and we wished to surprise you. He is to make the announcement of Millie's betrothal."

"This is a marvelous surprise!" Vanessa greeted Charles warmly. But when she noticed who was pushing the chair, her smile faltered a bit. It was Stephen.

"Vanessa." Charles smiled and reached out for her hand. "You look lovely this evening. And, Millie, my dearest, you are a vision."

Millie rushed over to plant a kiss on Charles's cheek. "Are you truly going to announce my engagement?"

"I am." Charles beamed at her. "You brother has most graciously given me that honor. Do I look presentable?"

Millie nodded quickly. "I have never seen you wear formal clothing before, and Aunt Lolly has not exaggerated. You are wickedly dashing!"

"Wickedly dashing?" Charles chuckled, highly amused at the phrase. "You'd best not let your fiancé hear your comment."

Millie giggled, exchanging fond glances with Lord Holmsby. "But he is wickedly dashing, also. I have told him so countless times."

While the conversation flowed on around her, Vanessa risked a glance at Stephen. She found him staring at her, and she drew a deep breath. It would be rude of her not to speak to him. She must do so with all haste.

"Good evening, Stephen." Vanessa's voice trembled slightly.

"Good evening, Vanessa." Stephen nodded back. "You are in fine looks this evening."

"Thank you." Vanessa felt a blush rise to her cheeks and she lowered her eyes. Though both Charles and Lord

Holmsby did look handsome in their formal wear, Stephen was the one who was wickedly dashing.

"Will you all join me as I make the announcement?" Charles smiled at them. "You are my family, and I should like to have you around me."

There were nods all around, and the small procession entered the ballroom. There was a moment of silence as the guests caught sight of Charles in his Bath chair, but he waved and several gentlemen immediately rushed over to offer their greetings. In a shorter time than Vanessa had thought possible, the converse resumed its former volume. She gave an audible sigh of relief. She heard several comments that praised Charles's courage, and several more exclaiming how fit he looked and how good it was to have him back among them once again. Charles's reentry into society had been accomplished quite handily, and it had not been the ordeal he had feared.

"Come, my dears." Charles waved away his friends, promising to speak to them later in the evening, and then he motioned their small group forward. "Let us take our places on the dais, and I shall make our happy announcement."

Vanessa hung back, intending to slip quietly into the crowd. She had no place on the dais with Charles and his family. But Aunt Lolly noticed her hesitation and pulled her forward. "Come along, Vanessa. You are a part of this family, too."

Once they had all achieved the dais, with the aid of a clever ramp fashioned to accommodate the Bath chair, Charles called for his silver-tipped cane and made his way to the podium without assistance. Once he had accomplished this act, several of their guests burst into spontaneous applause, calling out their congratulations for a job well done.

"Thank you, friends." Charles smiled at the assemblage of friends and guests. "I have three announcements I must make to you this evening. One is sad, so I shall do that first. I must inform you that my daughter, Phoebe, met her death in a carriage accident two years past, in Italy. I regret I have not informed you of this sooner, but my dear son-in-law, Stephen, and my own darling wife kept this painful news a secret, fearing it would reach my ears and I would suffer a relapse. They were quite right to do so, and I commend them for their compassion. Phoebe was but a brief candle, and now her light is gone."

Sympathetic murmurs filled the ballroom, and Charles was the recipient of many compassionate expressions. But then he smiled, and the sadness eased among the guests.

"And now, my friends, I have a second announcement to make, and it is extremely happy news. Most of you have met Stephen's sister, Millie, and you have also made the acquaintance of Lord Holmsby." Charles paused as the crowd began to murmur, and he laughed. "Undoubtedly you have already guessed what I am about to say. I am pleased to announce Millie and Lord Holmsby are to be wed. And from the fond looks I have witnessed, it cannot be too soon to suit them both."

There was good-natured laughter among the guests and several calls of congratulations. Then Charles quieted them with an upraised hand and prepared to speak again.

"And now for my third announcement, one that will undoubtedly take most of you by surprise. I am also pleased to inform you of another engagement in my dear family, between Miss Vanessa Holland and my son-in-law, Lord Bridgeford."

Vanessa gasped and turned to stare at Charles in shock. Whatever had possessed him to tell a bouncer like that? Then, as she realized all eyes were upon her, she forced a smile, even though she was so embarrassed she wished the dais would open up beneath her and send her tumbling out of sight.

"No doubt they appear quite shocked by my announcement." Charles chuckled as he turned to face them. "Vanessa and Stephen did not fathom that I knew of their plans to marry, and they had thought to keep their delightful secret for a time, so as not to steal your attention from Millie and Lord Holmsby. But there is good reason I have taken it upon myself to announce this second happy engagement. My dear wife and I wish to host a double wedding for Millie and John and Vanessa and Stephen before the Season is out. All in attendance here tonight shall be invited."

The audience applauded and Charles gave a little bow. When his guests had quieted, he resumed his speech. "And now that I have concluded my announcements, I ask the orchestra to play a suitable waltz so these two newly engaged couples may take the floor to open our very special Valentine's Day Ball."

Vanessa's feet seemed rooted to the spot, and she did not think she could move. But Stephen reached out to take her arm and she found she was walking down the ramp, moving toward the dance floor.

"Smile, Vanessa. We must not embarrass Charles."

Stephen's voice was low in her ear, but it held a note of command. Vanessa smiled obediently and then caught a glimpse of Stephen's stern countenance. "You had best take your own advice, sir, and arrange your lips accordingly."

"You are quite right." Stephen nodded, forcing his mouth into the semblance of a smile. "Whatever possessed you to ask Charles to announce our engagement?"

Vanessa's eyebrows shot up in surprise, and she had all she could do to maintain her smile. "I did not ask him to do so. I had thought he only wished to announce *Millie's* engagement. Indeed, I cannot understand why he should have done such a thing."

"Nor can I. But I fear we shall be forced to play along with his scheme, at least for the present."

Vanessa dipped her head in a nod. "Indeed, we must. I should not like to ruin Millie and John's engagement ball by causing a scene. And I would die before I would humiliate Charles."

"Then you will agree to marry me, rather than contradict Charles's announcement?"

There was a sparkle of humor deep in Stephen's blue eyes, and Vanessa responded by laughing softly. "No, Stephen. I said I would die rather than humiliate Charles. I did *not* say that I would marry you."

"Becoming my wife is a fate worse than death, then?"

Vanessa was about to tender a witty retort when she saw a flicker of pain cross Stephen's face. He had just learned his wife was dead—the wife who had used their marriage as an escape and made a mockery of their vows. She could not hurt him further. Her pride did not matter in the face of his well-being. She sighed and then looked into his eyes. "No, Stephen. Marriage to you would be the best of all possible things. If it were possible to set aside our differences, I should be most honored to be your wife."

Just then, to Vanessa's great relief, the orchestra struck up their waltz. She went into Stephen's arms and danced the familiar steps, hoping he would not hate her for the telling statement she had just made.

"I must hold you closer." Stephen's arms tightened around her, pulling her closer to his broad chest. "And you must look up at me and sigh in supreme happiness. We must appear, for all the world, as a couple most deeply in love."

Vanessa looked up at him, as he had bid her to do, and then her breath caught in her throat. "That should not be difficult, for I do love you with all my heart."

"As I love you." Stephen smiled down at her, his first real smile of the evening. "Surely you know that, Vanessa. If only I had not behaved so badly the last time we met."

Vanessa sighed, reaching up to touch his cheek. "You

must not be so stern with yourself, for I also behaved badly. Half the fault must be placed at my door."

"I have been in agony over my indiscretion. Do you think you could find it in your heart to forgive me?"

Vanessa smiled, touching his lips with her finger. "Hush, Stephen. I have already forgiven you. Can you also forgive me?"

"There is nothing to forgive, my love. I should be the happiest man in the world tonight if our engagement were real."

Vanessa, who had never before stumbled in Stephen's arms, did so now. But Stephen caught her expertly and she stared up at him with widened eyes. "Is this true? Or are you merely speaking sweet words in an attempt to make us appear more loving to the *ton*?"

"It is true, Vanessa." Stephen's smile grew wider and a familiar gleam appeared deep in his eyes. "Charles has done my work for me, but will you accept my belated proposal and become my wife?"

"You truly want to marry me?" Vanessa felt quite light-headed, so dizzy with her love for him she could scarcely believe her own ears.

"With all my heart."

He made as if to kiss her then, in full sight of the crush in the ballroom. But at the last moment, he whirled her out onto the darkened balcony and took possession of her lips.

Vanessa breathed his name and her arms rose to encircle his neck in a loving embrace. Their kiss burned a path of joy through her trembling body and Vanessa, who had never been missish in her life, felt as if she were about to swoon with the wonder of it all. Stephen wanted her for his wife. And, oh, how she wanted to spend the remainder of her life safe in his loving arms.

Their kiss lasted until the last notes of the waltz. They would not have noticed if the whole assemblage at the ball had peered through the windows to observe them, for their thoughts were only for each other. When Stephen lifted his lips from hers at last, Vanessa sighed in supreme happiness.

"You must say it, Vanessa. Do you accept my proposal?"

"Yes, Stephen, I accept." Vanessa's smile was golden. "But there is one bit of unfinished business I must accomplish before I am free to become your wife."

Stephen frowned slightly. "What would that be, my love?"

"I must find my secret admirer, who promised to be here tonight, and return his gold heart to him. It is only right I tell him I am in love with you."

"He knows your heart is already engaged." Stephen chuckled slightly. "All who are present tonight have heard the announcement Charles made."

"You are quite right, of course, but I must afford him the courtesy of returning his lovely gift. My only obstacle shall be identifying him from among the guests."

Stephen began to smile broadly. "I do not think that will present a problem, my love. You see, you have already met your secret admirer."

"I have?" Vanessa stared up at him in shock. "But who is he? And how do you know him? You must tell me his name."

"His name is Stephen Thurston, ninth Earl of Bridgeford."

Vanessa's eyes widened and then she began to smile. "*You* are my secret admirer, Stephen?"

"I am." Stephen nodded and bent down to kiss the tip of her nose. "I did not know I was free to court you, my darling, and I could not hold secret my love for you. I burned to tell you I loved you, but I could not speak of my passion to you. Instead, I put my tender words to paper in my letters to you."

"You thought my hair was like rays of golden sunlight?"

Vanessa began to giggle as she remembered some of his flowery phrases.

Stephen laughed. "I did, most truly. I still do, but now the rays are much shorter."

"And you believed my lips were the color of wild strawberries?"

"Indeed, they are." Stephen nodded. "Of course, I do not recall ever seeing a wild strawberry, but I am certain they would be that particular hue."

"But you wrote that my ankle was slim, and we both know that it is quite sturdy."

"Perhaps, but that does not matter to the poet within me." Stephen laughed and held her firmly. "My letters were the only way I had to keep you near me when I was away, Vanessa. Every word I wrote to you was from my heart."

"They were lovely words, Stephen. No one has ever spoken to me so, in voice or in a letter. Your sentiments sustained me when I was lonely and caused me to feel I was the object of some fine gentleman's affection."

"You were the object of my affection, and you always shall be." Stephen reached into his pocket, pulling out a small, velvet-covered casket. "And to prove I am, indeed, your secret admirer, I have a present for you. It is the gem I promised you in my last letter. We shall take it to the jeweler on the morrow and have it set into the heart."

Vanessa gasped at the shining emerald that lay against the silk lining. Then she turned her face up for his kiss. "You are my secret admirer, now and for always—and I did not know it until this very moment. What a merry chase our love has led us. and what a charming story we shall have to tell to our children."

"Yes, indeed." Stephen leaned down and brushed her lips with his. "And shall we have many children, my dearest love?"

Vanessa smiled a secret smile, nestling her head against

his warm chest. "I should imagine we shall, for I give you fair warning I intend to practice the art of making them until we have obtained absolute perfection."

ABOUT THE AUTHOR

Kathryn Kirkwood lives with her family in Granada Hills, California. Kathryn loves to hear from her readers, and you may write to her c/o Zebra Books. She also writes short contemporary romances for Zebra's Bouquet line as Gina Jackson. Her newest contemporary, *Cookies and Kisses*, will be published in February 2000. Please include a self-addressed stamped envelope if you wish a response. You may also contact her at her E-mail address: OnDit@aol.com. Or visit her Web sit at:

http://lilacs.homepage.com.

BOOK YOUR PLACE ON OUR WEBSITE AND MAKE THE READING CONNECTION!

We've created a customized website just for our very special readers, where you can get the inside scoop on everything that's going on with Zebra, Pinnacle and Kensington books.

When you come online, you'll have the exciting opportunity to:

- View covers of upcoming books

- Read sample chapters

- Learn about our future publishing schedule (listed by publication month *and author*)

- Find out when your favorite authors will be visiting a city near you

- Search for and order backlist books from our online catalog

- Check out author bios and background information

- Send e-mail to your favorite authors

- Meet the Kensington staff online

- Join us in weekly chats with authors, readers and other guests

- Get writing guidelines

- AND MUCH MORE!

**Visit our website at
http://www.zebrabooks.com**

More Zebra Regency Romances